DEVIL'S FACE

A DANE MADDOCK ADVENTURE

DAVID WOOD
STEPHEN JOHN

Devil's Face
Copyright 2017, 2018 by David Wood
All rights reserved

Published by Adrenaline Press
www.adrenaline.press

Adrenaline Press is an imprint of Gryphonwood Press
www.gryphonwoodpress.com

Cover design by Matthew Williams

Edited by Sean Ellis and Melissa Bowersock

This book is a work of fiction. All characters are
products of the authors' imaginations or are used
fictitiously.

ISBN-13: 978-1-940095-86-8

ISBN-10: 1-940095-86-7

A dead man's riddle sets Maddock and Bones on a search for a lost treasure and into peril!

For nearly a century, treasure hunters have searched for the lost treasure of notorious gangster, Dutch Schultz. When Dane Maddock and Bones Bonebrake take up the search, they find themselves in a race against a dangerous enemy and in the crosshairs of deadly assassin.

Maddock and Bones must unravel the clues and survive a game of cat and mouse where failure could mean death.

Praise for The Dane Maddock Adventures!

"A great read that provides lots of action, and thoughtful insight as well, into strange realms that are sometimes best left unexplored." *Paul Kemprecos, author of Cool Blue Tomb*

"Dane and Bones.... Together they're unstoppable. Rip-roaring action from start to finish. Wit and humor throughout. Just one question - how soon until the next one? Because I can't wait." *Graham Brown, author of Shadows of the Midnight Sun*

"David Wood has done it again. Quest takes you on an expedition that leads down a trail of adventure and thrills!" *David L. Golemon, Author of the Event Group series*

BOOKS and SERIES by DAVID WOOD

Arcanum
Magus
Brainwash
Herald
Maug

Jade Ihara Adventures (with Sean Ellis)
Oracle
Changeling
Exile

Bones Bonebrake Adventures
Primitive
The Book of Bones
Skin and Bones
Venom

Jake Crowley Adventures (with Alan Baxter)
Blood Codex
Anubis Key

Brock Stone Adventures
Arena of Souls
Track of the Beast (forthcoming)

Myrmidon Files (with Sean Ellis)
Destiny
Mystic

Sam Aston Investigations (with Alan Baxter)
Primordial
Overlord

PROLOGUE

Alex Singer turned left onto East Park Street and drove three blocks before seeing the awning on the right side of the road.

Palace Chop House Sea Food, Draught Beer, the disjointed sign read. The building was solid brick, with a single window to the left of the entrance. Just beyond the restaurant was a parking lot.

Fifteen cents to park? Singer thought as he pulled his black 1933 Ford Coupe into the lot. He shook his head. Charging money to park your car—what was this country turning into?

He opened the car door and stepped out of the vehicle, carefully looking in all directions to see if he was being watched. Convinced he was not, Singer casually strolled through the parking lot and around the corner. He noted two young men wearing fedoras and dark business suits standing near the front door of the building. Neither seemed to look his way or gave the slightest indication they were aware of his presence.

He walked under a canopy that read, *Dine Dance, Steaks & Chops, Palace, Sea Food - Draught Beer*. A hand-written sign taped to the window read: *Closed for cleaning*. Singer continued through the door, checking his watch. It was quarter of eleven. He was a little early.

Singer instantly spotted the man he'd come to see. He sat alone at the far end of the room, facing the door with his back positioned against the wall, presumably so no one could sneak in from behind and surprise him. There were two other men standing in the restaurant, remaining near the doorway—bodyguards.

The man nodded in acknowledgment when he made eye contact. He stood and motioned Singer to join him. The table was clear with the exception of a glass of water and a single metal ashtray, overflowing with cigarette butts.

"Dutch Schultz?" he asked, though he knew very well who the man was. *The Dutchman*, as he was sometimes called, was one of the deadliest and most wanted gangsters in the country.

"I'm Alex Singer."

One of the bodyguards moved in. "Hands in the air, Mr. Singer," he said.

Singer grimaced, displeased with the idea of being searched. The bodyguard paused.

"Sorry," Schultz said. "This is Lulu. It's his job. He needs to frisk you. Can't be too careful."

Singer complied, raising his arms. The bodyguard searched him carefully, stepping back and nodding at the Dutchman.

Schultz had short, dark, oiled hair, neatly combed, parted on the left side. His face was oval, framing his buggy dark eyes, thin lips and bent nose. He wore a dark three-piece business suit and a long gray wool overcoat. A tan fedora with a dark band sat on the table to his right. Singer knew Schultz to be only thirty-three years old, but his careworn appearance made him look ten years older. He had no idea what his sister saw in the man who sat before him.

Singer pointed at the chair opposite Schultz and extended his hand. "May I?" he continued.

Shultz took a long draw on his cigarette and sized up the man standing in front of him. After a few seconds, he exhaled a large plume of smoke and gave a slight head nod toward the chair, inviting him to sit. He then made eye contact with each of the bodyguards and nodded. Both men moved to the front of the restaurant, outside of earshot.

Singer and Schultz both sat. Schultz's eyes were fixed on him, as if deciding whether or not he was trustworthy.

"Draught beer?" Singer said. He pronounced it phonetically as 'draut.'

Schultz twisted his face in a confused expression. "What?" he asked. "You want a beer?"

"No," Singer replied. "Your sign out front. It says *Draught Beer.*"

"It's pronounced 'droft,'" Schultz replied. "It's the same as 'draft.' You know, like draft beer."

"Why not just say 'draft?'" Singer wanted to know.

Schultz looked mildly irritated. "Hell, I don't know. It's German, I think. The sign was already up when I set up shop. I didn't put it up."

"I haven't seen the word 'draught' since I served in the war," he said, this time pronouncing it correctly. "I never actually heard the word spoken out loud before."

Schultz showed no reaction. "I understand you were in the Great War. She said you saw major action. You were in the First Battle of the Marne? Right?"

"The *Second* Battle of the Marne," he corrected. "In 1918. We joined the French and the British against a massive German assault. Twenty-three German divisions moved into the Marne, near Paris. I was one of 85,000 American soldiers brought in to help turn the tide."

"A lot of men died in that battle," Schultz said, nodding.

"On both sides," Singer replied. "Nearly 140,000 men died or were seriously wounded, including 12,000 Americans."

"And you received the Distinguished Service Cross and the Silver Star," Schultz said. "Your sister is very proud of you."

Singer nodded.

"I heard you faced enemy fire to save a wounded captain," the Dutchman continued.

"It's all in a day's work," Singer replied. "He would have done the same for me."

Schultz shook his head. "But you lived through it. Came out stronger as a result, I suspect. I guess that explains why you don't look the least bit intimidated at being here with me."

Singer nodded. "When you've lived through the horrors of war, it's hard to be intimidated by a man in a chair, no matter who the man is."

Schultz nodded and fell silent for a moment.

"Fair enough," he said. "How is she?"

"My sister is heartbroken, as you can imagine," Singer replied.

"I know. I'm sorry." He slid an envelope across the table. It was three inches thick. "This should help."

Singer picked it up and opened it. The envelope was filled with cash. How much, he didn't know, but it looked like a tidy sum, perhaps five thousand dollars, maybe even more.

"Thank you," he said, wondering what kind of man believed the only thing that could help a woman's broken heart was money. "It will help, but it's not all about money, you know. She loves you."

Schultz shrugged. "I can't be around her. None of the people who are after me know about her. That's the way it needs to stay. It's for her own safety. Things are complicated right now. I got a lotta heat on me."

Singer knew this already. Between what he'd read in the papers and what his sister had told him, he knew a great deal about the man sitting before him. Dutch Schultz had the distinction of being named Public Enemy Number One by the Justice Department in 1933. Rumor had it that Schultz had killed or ordered the deaths of one hundred thirty-six people over the last ten years. The gangster promised his sister that he would divorce his wife and be with her, but of course, it was an empty promise. He also knew he was looking at a dead man. The person sitting across the table from him had made very powerful enemies on both sides of the law and the end of the line was not far away.

U.S. Attorney Thomas Dewey was hot after him for tax evasion, according to the papers. Schultz decided the only way to get Dewey off his back was to kill him. He had gone to the Mafia Commission, headed by none other than Lucky Luciano himself, and asked for permission to carry out a hit on Dewey. Luciano thought the hit was too risky and would draw too much heat to his organization. He declined to sanction the execution, but Schultz, being Schultz, ignored him and publicly threatened to kill the man anyway.

Schultz also confided to his sister that Lucky had put out a contract with mobster Lepke Buchalter to *handle things*—meaning to kill Schultz. Luciano had been furious that his orders were being ignored. That was when Dutch cut ties with the woman he loved—for her protection. The money Alex Singer now held was undoubtedly guilt money.

"I heard about your complications," Singer said, understating the situation. "Thanks for leaving my sister out of it."

Dutch shrugged. "She's a good woman. She didn't sign up for this."

"How much time before they come after you?" he asked.

"I don't know," came the reply. "I have bodyguards protecting me around the clock."

"But it will happen, sooner rather than later?"

"Yeah," Dutch said. "Maybe in a week, maybe a month, I don't know."

Singer stood. "Anything else?" he asked.

"Yes," Dutch replied. He reached over and retrieved a book off the empty seat to his right. He handed it to Singer.

The war veteran looked it over. A confused look formed on his face. "*Mary Poppins?*"

"What?" Schultz replied. "You don't like kid stuff?"

Singer chuckled. "Excuse me for saying so, Mr. Schultz, but I would not have taken you to be the reading sort, and even if you were, you don't exactly look like a Mary Poppins kind of guy."

An odd expression formed on Schultz's face. At first Singer thought he had insulted the famous gangster. But after a moment, the tiniest of smiles formed on his face. He shrugged.

"It's for her. A birthday gift. It was a few days ago. She probably thinks I forgot. She mentioned to me that she'd been wanting to read it. It's a first edition. Will you make sure she gets it?"

The man nodded. "Of course."

Did Schultz even know his sister was pregnant? Singer didn't think so but the book made him wonder. It was something a mother might read to a child.

He opened the book and looked at the inside cover. Dutch had written an inscription inside:

Happy Birthday
10-19-1910
I wish I could have kept you… safe.

Singer looked at Dutch. "The date…it's my sister's birthdate. She was born in 1910, on October nineteen."

"That's right."

"What are all these notes in the margins of the pages?" Singer asked, flipping through the pages of the book.

"Just random things," Schultz said, shrugging. "Things she and I shared—they will have meaning to her."

"See what the devil sees?" Singer read aloud. "That's something you shared with my sister? This will have meaning to her?"

Dutch looked mildly annoyed. "Your sister will understand, all right?"

Singer shrugged and tucked the book under his arm. He carefully placed the envelope filled with money inside his left breast pocket and backed away.

"Good luck to you," he said.

"Don't lose that book," Dutch admonished. "It's more important than you know."

"I won't lose it," Singer insisted.

"Tell your sister …" Dutch fell silent.

"Tell her what?" Singer asked.

"Tell her... that I'm sorry about... about everything."

"Will do." Singer tipped his hat and left the restaurant.

Fifteen minutes later Dutch Schultz finished his business at the urinal in the restroom and flushed. He was at the sink washing his hands when he heard the sound of gunshots exploding from the direction of the dining room. Inside the confines of the restaurant the shots boomed like cannon fire.

Dutch drew his pistol. He knew they were going to come after him soon, but this was sooner than expected.

He heard the sounds of glass exploding; wood splintering; men crying out in pain. Dutch had lost count of how many rounds had been fired. The gunfire finally ceased. He leveled his pistol at the door and waited. The battle was clearly finished, but who had survived? His men, or the assassins who had come for him?

Thirty seconds passed. Forty-five. A full minute. Finally, Dutch called to his two bodyguards. "Lulu! Bernard! Are you okay?"

He heard footsteps, but no reply came. His gun was still trained on the bathroom entrance. He saw something through the crack at the bottom of the door. Whoever was outside the door was just standing there.

"Who's there?" Dutch demanded.

"It's Charles Workman," came the reply. "We've met."

"Yeah, I remember," Dutch screamed. "You're one of Lepke's stooges. Where's your pal, Mendy?"

"I'm here, too," came the reply of another voice. The two men chuckled. "Sorry, Dutch. Lepke says we gotta do this. It wasn't my choice. Why don't you come on out? We'll make it quick and easy, I promise."

"The only thing I've ever done quick and easy was your mother last night," Dutch replied, and then fired three shots into the door.

The door flew open, and Mendy and Charles burst inside, each firing as they moved. Both shots missed. Schultz fired off two rounds of his own, but he did so while ducking away and the shots were wildly off target. Mendy corrected his aim and fired again. Dutch felt the impact of the bullet bursting through the center of his chest. He clutched his chest, feeling the hot blood on his fingers, and slumped to the floor. Mendy took aim at Dutch's head and pulled the trigger. He heard a loud click but there was no gunshot. The pistol was empty. In the distance a police siren could be heard.

"C'mon, let's get outta here," Charles said. "We made a lot of racket. The police are coming."

Mendy looked at Dutch. A bloody circle formed around him, growing slowly larger.

"He's finished. Let's move!" Charles insisted.

Mendy nodded and followed Charles from the room.

Dutch wasn't finished. Clinging to consciousness and knowing he was mortally wounded the first thought that came to his head was getting out of the bathroom and back to the diner. Proud until the end, he did not want the headlines to read, "*Dutch Schultz found dead under urinal.*"

He struggled to his feet, nearly passing out in the process. By sheer will alone, he managed to stagger out of the restroom and into the dining room where he saw the corpses of his two bodyguards, Lulu and Bernard. He shuffled over to the seat where he had spoken to Alex Singer just moments earlier, and sat, setting his hat neatly in place. Then, he slumped forward, laying his head on the table. The sirens grew louder.

Dutch was still conscious when the police barged into the restaurant, though his head never moved from the table.

"That's Dutch Shultz over there," he heard one of the cops say. "Is he dead?"

Dutch felt little pain—he was in shock, confused and disoriented. He felt warm fingers touching his neck.

"He's still alive but his pulse is really weak," another voice said. "Look at all this blood. It's everywhere."

"Dutch! Dutch!" a third voice called out. "There ain't no way you're livin' through this one. You're almost gone. You have to tell us. Who did this to you?"

Dutch lifted his head weakly. His mouth moved. He spoke; his words were barely a whisper. "A boy has never wept... nor dashed a thousand kim."

ONE

Uriah "Bones" Bonebrake took a peek at his hole cards – ace, king, both hearts. It was one of the best starting hands in Texas Hold'em. It was certainly the best hand he'd been dealt all night and he had been sitting at the table for more than five hours.

They were playing in the Poker Room at the Borgata, in Atlantic City, never short on high-rollers with money to burn. It was 2:30 a.m. Friday night—or technically Saturday morning—and the place was still packed. Poker players from all walks of life were testing their skills against each other. Men, women, young, old, and a veritable United Nations of nationalities. It was a melting pot of humanity, and Bones—a six-and-a-half-foot-tall Cherokee Indian—was melting right in with everyone else. He wasn't a high-roller and he didn't have money to burn, but gambling was in his blood. His uncle, Crazy Charlie, had made his fortune running the tribal casino.

Bones enjoyed gambling, taking big chances for high stakes, and he took it very seriously, despite the sometimes raunchy humor he employed as a defense mechanism. He wasn't living on the edge financially, but he wasn't exactly rolling in the dough. His work as a professional treasure hunter—partnered with his former Navy SEAL teammate, Dane Maddock—had the potential to be very lucrative and indeed, he and Maddock had made some pretty amazing discoveries, but the really big paydays were few and far between. He could afford to lose, but he couldn't afford to be reckless.

He was the "big blind," meaning he would be the last player to bet. Of the eight other players at the table, five had already folded. The sixth player, a sturdily built man with close-cropped gray hair, clad in a Honda shirt, called the bet, tossing in fifty dollars' worth of chips. The seventh player, a tiny middle-aged Asian woman dripping in diamonds and pearls, called as well. The eighth player, a barrel-chested cowboy-type, his cheap Walmart shirt stretched to its limits by his barrel chest, raised the bet to one hundred fifty and sneered at Bones.

Bones scoffed. "You bet like a chick."

The cowboy was quick with a comeback. "This chick has been kicking your ass all night."

Bones didn't reply. He stared at the pot.

"Sir," the dealer said. "The bet is to you."

"There ain't no peace pipe being passed around here, Tonto," the cowboy said. "Make a decision, will you?"

Bones fiercely disliked the cowboy. He had a distinct redneck vibe about him, and Bones hated rednecks. What was more, the jerk had been winning all night, him in his stupid oversized cowboy hat that had probably never seen an actual ranch. In head to head matchups, the cowboy had taken Bones down four straight times. This hand would be different, he thought. "Don't cry," Bones said. "You'll ruin your mascara."

"I ain't the one with the pretty ponytail."

"I'm not surprised you think it's pretty," Bones shot back.

Then he raised the bet from one-fifty to three hundred.

Bones averted his eyes from the cowboy, not wanting to give away any indication that he held a strong starting hand. He checked his watch.

The dealer burned a card and flipped over three cards, an ace, a king and a nine, all suited differently. It was a great flop for Bones who now held two pair, aces and kings. Outwardly he showed no emotion whatsoever, but inside he was eager to let out a massive war whoop.

The tiny Asian woman checked the bet. Cowboy ignored her and fixed his stare on Bones. Arms folded, he studied Bones' face, looking for a reaction.

"What's the problem? Trying to count higher than ten without taking off your shoes?" Bones taunted.

The man in the Honda shirt chuckled.

"Bite me," the cowboy replied, looking at his hole cards once again.

Bones smirked. "I don't like waiting in long lines."

"The bet is to you, sir," the dealer said.

Cowboy took one last look at Bones and reached into his stack of chips, tossing several of them onto the table directly in front of him.

"The bet is one thousand," the dealer said.

Several 'oohs' and "ahhhs' could be heard as people from the casino started to gather around the table to watch the drama unfold.

Bones could hardly contain his excitement. He figured the old fart for a pair of aces—maybe even with a high kicker, but not two pair. He was ready to take down his opponent. He could feel it. This would be the hand that made his whole night worthwhile. Certain he was ahead, he was eager to raise the bet, but he pretended to consider his options, hoping to lure the cowboy into deeper betting. He sighed, scratched his head, let out a breath.

If Maddock were here now he would have been applauding the dramatic performance.

More people continued to gather around the table

once the dealer called out a bet of that size. All the better for Bones. He had been playing second fiddle to the cowboy all night and wanted nothing more than to take him down in front of a crowd.

Bones tapped his fingers as if he were deeply contemplating whether he would call the bet or not, milking the moment for dramatic effect. Out of the corner of his eye he saw an attractive woman standing about ten feet away. He decided she was worth a second, longer look. Auburn hair, green eyes, curvy, cute—and smiling at him.

He smiled back but only for a moment. He needed to focus on the matter at hand. He looked again at the cowboy.

"I think white man speaks with forked tongue," he said, with faux Native American gravitas.

"So, whatcha gonna do?" the cowboy asked, getting anxious. "You gonna call? Or are you gonna fold?"

"I'm thinking," Bones said in his normal voice. "I'm Cherokee. We like to sit around the campfire, taking a few hits off the old peace pipe, conjuring spirits, drinking firewater, getting the munchies...."

"Well, make a decision sometime in this century, would you?"

"Just wondering, cowboy," he replied. "Have you ever been to Little Big Horn?"

"No," the cowboy said.

"That's too bad," Bones replied.

The comment elicited a ripple of laughter from the gathering crowd.

The cowboy rolled his eyes. "That was the Sioux and Cheyenne tribes, not the Cherokee."

"You're a real buzz-kill, you know that?" Bones fired

back. He turned to the Asian woman. "And you! You remember Pearl Harbor."

The woman frowned. "I am Chinese. Not Japanese."

"Don't bore me with details."

"My shirt's Japanese," Honda quipped. Everyone chuckled.

"How about it, Tonto?" the cowboy said.

"Okay, everyone keep quiet, will you?" Bones snapped. "I'm tryin' to concentrate here."

Finally, Bones called, placing a thousand dollars in chips into the pot, proud at the portrayal of reluctance he displayed. The Asian woman called as well.

The pot was now just over six thousand.

The fourth card, called "the turn," was a seven. It was very unlikely that the card helped anyone at the table.

Bones smiled at the cowboy and said, "All in," pushing the remaining chips—his last two thousand—into play. The crowd, which had now grown even larger, gasped when they saw all the chips go into the pot.

The woman who had been checking him out moved in closer, Bones noticed. He could actually smell her fragrance. It reminded him of honeysuckle.

The Asian woman called, which surprised Bones a bit, but not overly so. She had been betting recklessly all night. She had Bones' bet more than covered, but pushed all her chips forward as well, calling *all in*, too.

The cowboy looked nervous but called the bet anyway. He knew he was screwed, Bones thought, but the cowboy was in too deep to pull away now. There was now just over twelve thousand in the pot. With Bones and the Asian woman both all in, the betting for the hand concluded and the dealer instructed the players to turn up their cards before the final card, called, "the river," was dealt.

Bones proudly turned over his ace/king. The cowboy sighed heavily and barked an expletive, flipping over his ace/ten. The Asian woman had pocket jacks.

Bones flattened his hand and patted his mouth several times, making the obligatory, '*Woo, Woo, Woo*' stereotypical Native American war whoop.

The crowd ooh'd and ahh'd, sensing Bones' victory.

"Screw you," the cowboy huffed.

"You're drawing dead, my friend," Bones snapped. In poker, the term *drawing dead* meant there was no card left in the deck that could be turned that would allow the cowboy to win. Even if the last card was a ten, the cowboy's two pair would be lower than Bones' two pair. The Asian woman had pocket jacks. That meant there were only two cards remaining in the deck that could beat him—one of the final jacks. The odds against one of those cards coming up were high.

Bones stood, preparing to give a whooping war dance to celebrate his victory.

"Settle down, Tonto," the cowboy huffed.

"Hey cowboy!" he barked. "Tonto was a Potawatamie, not a Cherokee."

The cowboy let out a low groan. "Jerk," he muttered.

The dealer dealt the final card. The lady had just hit a set of jacks. Bones groaned when he saw the jack turn up. The Asian woman let out a howl of excitement, standing and flailing her arms in the air. "I win! I win!"

The people standing around the table cheered for her. The cowboy raised both of his hands over his head and began a long, slow clap that lasted long after the crowd noise died down.

"That's what you get, smartass," the cowboy

snapped. "Put that in your peace pipe and smoke it."

"Pardon me, cowboy, but isn't that you who just got your ass handed to you right alongside me," Bones said.

"Yeah? But for me the look on your face made the whole thing worth it. I'm gonna walk over to the window and sign a little slip of paper and get five thousand more in chips from my line of credit. You want to come with me so you can get yours, too?"

Bones sat there, scowling.

"Yeah, I didn't think so," the cowboy said.

"Assclown," Bones muttered as the man walked away. His stomach was in knots and he thought he was going to vomit then and there. He sat there, watching the dealer push all the chips toward the Chinese woman. She looked at Bones, holding up several chips, rubbing them together, and chortled. "Hee, hee, hee."

"What were you even doing in the hand after the flop?" Bones asked, irritated.

"I had two jacks," she replied.

"Yes I know but, there was an ace and a king on the flop," Bones replied. "The cowboy and I were both betting our asses off. You had to know that one or both of us had at least a pair higher than your jacks."

"So?"

"So?" he repeated. "Are you serious?"

"I am a brave woman," she said.

"You're just lucky."

"Keep your bra on, sissy," she snapped.

Bones sighed. "Better lucky than good, I guess."

"Here," she called out, tossing a twenty-five dollar chip his way. "Go play the slots with the other little old ladies."

Several people in the crowd roared with laughter.

Bones couldn't help but laugh, although, as he stood and walked away, he wondered how the casino management might feel if he scalped the lady right then and there.

Twenty minutes later, Bones sat at the nickel slot machines, nursing a watered-down Diet Coke, feeding the one-armed bandit. He first saw her reflection in the shiny chrome frame of the slot machine. It was the beautiful woman who'd been watching him at the poker tables. She was standing behind him.

"How about I buy you a real adult beverage?" she asked. "It looks like you could use it."

Bones turned to face her. Up close she was even cuter than he originally thought. Her long auburn hair, shapely figure and full lips gave her a vibe he really liked. As disturbed as he was over losing all his money, he couldn't help but smile at her.

"Cool with me," he replied. "To what do I owe this pleasure?"

"You're Uriah Bonebrake, right?" she asked.

"You've got me at a disadvantage."

"My name is Michelle Jensen," she replied, extending her hand.

"Seems you know my name already," he said.

"I do. I'm looking to meet Dane Maddock and I thought you could help," she said.

"But you and I are such a better match," Bones replied.

She smiled, her eyebrows raised. "Oh really? And why would that be?"

"Maddock has that boy next door thing going, I'll give you that, but I'm a hell of a lot better looking."

"I do like knuckle draggers, I have to admit. But I

like all sorts."

"Oh, did I mention that Maddock is, how should I say this, poorly endowed?" Bones said. "Seriously, it looks like a scared turtle down there."

Michelle laughed. "I won't ask how you know that. Seriously, though, I'm just here on business."

"Hmmm, monkey business, I hope," Bones said with a lecherous grin.

"No, *money* business."

"Ah, my *second* favorite kind of business," he said

"And I'd really like to meet Dane Maddock to discuss it," she said.

"And I'm certain he'd like to meet you," he said. He shook her hand. "Everyone calls me Bones. Except for my grandfather, and my mother when she's really pissed."

"Well, Bones," she said. "We have a lot to talk about."

TWO

Dane Maddock was watching the Atlanta Braves blow another big lead on one of the flat screen televisions at Harry's Oyster Bar on the Boardwalk when he saw Bones arrive.

Harry's Oyster Bar had only been opened since 2011 but carried a tradition dating back to 1897 when Dock's Oyster House first opened in Atlantic City. The name came from the original owner, Harry "Dock" Dougherty, and ownership had been handed down through the family. The bar was located right on the Boardwalk. The décor was framed in mahogany millwork with maritime lighting focused on a massive multi-tiered shellfish display and a twenty-foot marble slab raw bar.

"I am gonna order myself a whole plate of the Wianno Cape Cod oysters," Bones said, taking a seat. "And I want a bowl of clam chowder."

He flagged a waitress and ordered, making an attempt to be funny and flirty with the heavily tattooed waitress; she was having none of it. He looked at Maddock and shrugged.

"After losing five large I'd think you'd order something a little less pricey," Maddock said.

"Hey, we only live once," replied Bones. "Besides, I don't have any money—you're buying."

"I figured. So, where is this hot girl you were telling me about?" Maddock asked.

Bones looked at his watch. "I told her to meet us here at seven o'clock. That's only a couple of minutes away. Just remember, I saw her first."

Maddock smiled. "I would not forget that. Tell me

about this woman, again."

Bones shrugged. "Nothing much to tell. I saw her watching me at the poker tables. After I lost my stack in a bad bet, she came up to me and said she wanted to meet you. Already knew my name and that you work for me."

Maddock ignored the wisecrack. "A bad beat?"

"C'mon man, who sits on jacks when an ace and a king come up on the flop and everyone is betting their butts off?"

"I guess fifty-year-old Chinese women do," he said.

"Whatever," Bones replied. "It was a bad beat."

"And how did this woman know where to find you?" Maddock asked.

"We have a mutual acquaintance," a female voice from behind said.

Maddock turned and saw Michelle for the first time. He stood. Bones had been right, he thought. This woman was stunning. She wore little or no makeup and certainly didn't need it. She wore skinny jeans and a tight-fitting white cotton top that accentuated all the right curves.

"Who shall I thank for the introduction?" Maddock asked.

"Kaylin Maxwell," she said. "She and I went to school together."

Maddock smiled. Kaylin was the daughter of his former SEAL Commander, Hartford "Maxie" Maxwell. It was Kaylin who had brought the news to him that Maxie had been murdered while seeking a biblical artifact, lost at sea on a nineteenth century sailing vessel called the *Dourado*.

"Please have a seat, Ms. Jensen," Maddock said, waving at the spot next to him.

"Thanks, and call me Michelle." She settled into the seat with a casual gracefulness. "I hear the oysters here are amazing."

"They are, and you're in luck," Bones said. "I'm going to have them bring over a plate full of them."

She smiled. "Good. I'm buying."

"Even better. I'll order *two* plates, then."

"So, how is Kaylin?" Maddock asked. The two had something of a history, but hadn't spoken in some time.

"Fine." The look on Michelle's face told him that was the only answer he was likely to receive.

The waitress brought Bones' clam chowder and set it in front of him.

"Thanks," he replied. "I forgot to order a spoon. Can you hook me up, or should I eat it like a cat?"

The waitress frowned and picked up a place setting from a different table and slapped it down beside the bowl. She flashed Bones a sour look, flipped him off with her middle finger and walked away.

"She wants me," Bones remarked.

"Yeah, that has to be it," Michelle replied.

"Why did you look us up?" Maddock asked.

"Kaylin tells me that you are seekers of lost relics and buried treasure," she said, "and that you're the best and, most importantly, you can be trusted."

He shrugged. "We've been known to…"

"I have a job that needs doing," she interrupted. "I'll warn you in advance. It will be out of the box for you."

"What do you mean, out of the box?" he asked.

"I know you typically search for treasures on old shipwrecks, cities of gold or secret scrolls. This job does not involve magic stones, mythical sea serpents, ancient pyramids, or lost cities. On the surface, this one will probably seem a little more... vanilla... mundane."

"What is the job?" Maddock asked.

"Safe-cracking," she said.

"So, when you say out of the box," Bones began, "you mean climbed out of the box, left the house, and drove to the other side of town."

"You're right, it's not our area of expertise," Maddock admitted.

"Before it can be opened, it has to be found," she replied. "That *is* your area of expertise."

"And inside the safe is...?" Bones asked.

"As much as seven million in cash or Liberty gold coins, or both, it's rumored," Michelle replied. "Perhaps other things, too."

"What do you mean, rumored?" Maddock asked.

"No one knows for sure," she said. "No one is even positive the safe exists."

Bones rolled his eyes. Michelle didn't catch it. Maddock did notice the eye roll, understood his friend's intent, and was in full agreement. This was sounding worse and worse as it went along.

"But *you* think it does exist?" he replied.

"I do," she said.

"Who did the safe belong to?" Bones asked.

"Dutch Schultz," she said.

Maddock sighed. "Oh boy," he said, trying not to allow a note of sarcasm to touch his voice.

He knew all about Dutch Schultz and the infamous hidden safe. There was not a treasure hunter in the world that didn't know the story. Schultz was a notorious gangster from the 1930s. He had been arrested for tax evasion but was acquitted. The way the legend was told, Schultz hid all his money and his valuables in tobacco sacks and stuffed them in a container: a safe, iron box or steel suitcase, and buried it in a secret place, until such time as conditions allowed him to recover it. Unfortunately, he was murdered the day after he was said to have buried his treasure. On his deathbed, he had made a number of statements, many of which were nonsensical and assumed to have been spoken in a feverish, delirious state. Every word he spoke had been analyzed over and over ad nauseum in an effort to decode some secret message as to the whereabouts of the safe he buried. In over eighty years of looking, no one had come close.

"I know the story," Maddock said. "I also know that hundreds of people have tried to find it. Some of them were pretty darn good archaeologists and treasure hunters."

"And then there was Grizzly Grant," Bones said quietly.

Maddock grinned. A sometimes television host, Grizzly had developed an undeserved reputation among conspiracy theorists, treasure hunters, and cryptozoologists as an expert in those fields. Despite that, he'd become something of a friend to Maddock and Bones. His attempt to find the safe had crashed and burned like so many of his endeavors.

"More like thousands of treasure hunters," Michelle admitted.

"I know the story, too," Bones added. "I also know that rumors of the hidden treasure never surfaced until after the man died. I never bought into the story myself."

"Really? Why is that?" she asked.

"Dutch Schultz was a con artist, a murderer and a thief," he said. "He trusted no one. All the clues he supposedly left were probably made just to throw people off track—one last *kiss my ass* before he checked out. I know people who tried—tried and failed. They were good men. They would have found the safe by now if it actually existed."

The smile on Michelle's face disappeared. "It does exist."

"You seem certain," Maddock said.

"I am certain," she replied.

"And you want to look for it?" Bones asked.

"Yes, I do. I actually believe what you said, Bones."

"You do?" he replied, incredulously. "Chicks don't normally say that to me. I never know why."

"Yeah, I wonder," she said turning back to Maddock. "I do think Dutch may very well have left false clues to intentionally throw people off track."

"Why do I feel there is a *but* coming?" Maddock asked.

"*But ...*" she continued, "what if Dutch left other clues privately to someone he *wanted* to find the safe? What if he left those clues to someone he loved? Clues that no one else knew about?"

Bones studied Michelle's face, as if trying to decide whether she was serious or not. "That would put a different spin on things, then, wouldn't it?" he finally said.

Maddock finished an oyster and took a swig of beer. "You haven't told us what your connection to all this is."

"Dutch Schultz was my great-grandfather," she replied. "My great-grandmother was not his wife," said Michelle. "She was his mistress. She was pregnant with my grandmother at the time of Dutch's death."

"So, your interest in this is personal, we get it,"

Bones said. "That doesn't make the facts of the situation any different. Like Maddock said, loads of skilled treasure hunters have tried to uncover the Dutchman's treasure, and no one has come close. I'm sorry, it's a waste of time."

"You're right," she said. "Hundreds, perhaps thousands of men have tried their hand at hunting down my great-grandfather's treasure. But ..."

She reached into her handbag and pulled out a book. She set it on the table and pushed it toward the two men.

"None of them had this."

THREE

Maddock picked up the book and inspected it. It was old, perhaps an original first edition. "*Mary Poppins?*" he noted, opening the inside cover, "published in 1934."

Bones frowned. "Let me guess, it's hidden in a chimney, or an umbrella. I haven't read the book," he added, "but I used to get drunk and mock the movie just to piss off my sister."

"Keep laughing," Michelle snapped. "You won't be laughing for long."

"I pegged you for more of a Harry Potter type," Bones said.

"Among other things, but can we focus, please?"

"You aren't actually buying into this, are you?" Bones asked Maddock.

Maddock had been reading the inscription. He turned the book around and slid it to Bones, who picked it up and read Dutch Schultz's words aloud.

"*Happy Birthday, I wish I could have kept you safe,*" he read. "And there's a date, but it says 1910? Schultz was killed in 1935."

"The date inscribed is my great-grandmother's birthday, 10-19-1910."

"Okay, well that's an odd inscription, I'll give you that—but so what?" Bones noted.

"He used the word *'safe'* in the inscription," Maddock replied.

Michelle nodded.

"It's a coincidence," Bones said.

Maddock flipped through the pages, "There's a note here in the margin, *Speaking of the Devil. He faces southeast.*"

"So?" Bones replied.

"Son-of-a-gun!" Maddock blurted out.

"Would one of you two mind sharing this revelation?" Bones asked.

"Devil… '*faces*' southeast. Makes me think of Devil's Face," Maddock said.

"I'm not following you," Bones replied.

"The Devil's Face rock formation in the New York Catskills was one of the more popular theories as to the location of the Dutchman's lost treasure. My parents retired to New York and I read about it in one of my dad's books." Maddock winced. Even after all these years, the memory of his parents still pained him.

"That could be coincidence," Bones said.

"The words *safe*, *Devil* and *face*—all written on the inside leaf?" Maddock snapped. "That can't be a coincidence."

"That was my thought," Michelle added. "This book was handed to my great-grandmother's brother literally minutes before he was murdered. He died on October twenty-third. He bought the book earlier that day. That means he wrote these comments a few hours after he buried his treasure."

"And just before he was killed. There are notes made in the margins throughout this book," Maddock said. "These notes were written by Dutch Schultz himself?"

"They are," Michelle said. "I believe this is far more than a book. I think it's a code that, when deciphered, becomes a map to the Dutchman's buried safe. I believe he was writing a code to communicate the location of his treasure to my great-grandmother—a code only she might understand."

"It sounds like horse crap to me," said Bones.

Michelle shook her head. "It isn't. His world was collapsing. Dutch Schultz knew he didn't have much time. The attorney general was hot on his trail and the Mafia Commission had ordered a hit on him. He was panicking."

"And no one else has ever seen this book before?" Bones asked.

"That's right," Michelle said, "just my great-grandmother, my grandmother, my mother and me, as it was handed down."

"If this book is authentic and these notations were truly written by the Dutchman, I'll grant you that it does make this whole thing very interesting," Maddock said, "but you realize that Devil's Face is already well known as one of the probable locations of the treasure. Every inch of the area has already been searched."

"I know," she said, "but flip through the book. There are notes written throughout many of the pages—clues. I need help deciphering them, and then finding the safe's location."

Maddock began to flip through the pages. There were at least two dozen handwritten notes written in the margins of the book. None of the notes were relevant to the Mary Poppins story. They seemed to be nothing more than idle ramblings.

"Read some of the notes," Bones said, his curiosity aroused.

"Read the note on page thirty-four," Michelle said. "It gets more interesting."

Maddock flipped to page thirty-four and read aloud, "*Maybe if Max had a Coke in the good old U.S.A. Hamas would have had a chance. His stock was on the rise until he fought Max in Nazi-land. Instead, it was a certified KO.*"

Bones scrunched his face. "What the hell does that mean?"

"KO is boxing slang for knockout," Maddock said.

"I know what KO means in boxing," Bones scoffed. "I've been knocked before, you know."

"*Max* could be a reference to Max Schmeling, a very famous boxer during the Dutchman's time," Michelle said, ignoring Bones' comment. "Dutch was a huge boxing fan. Who is Hamas, though?"

"I'm looking it up now on my cell," Maddock said.

Bones picked up the book. "I can't get past these handwritten notes in the margins throughout the book," he said, thumbing through the pages. "Listen to this: *When I see you at Christmas we'll take in the countryside. The train ride has beautiful scenery. I love red.*"

"I wonder if this is truly a clue?" Maddock asked.

Michelle shrugged. "I think that particular note may be misdirection. There is no train that intersected his drive from New York to New Jersey."

"What the hell does *I love red* mean?" Bones asked. "He was talking about the scenery. Is he talking about the leaves changing color in the fall?"

"I thought so at first," Michelle said, "but he mentions Christmas time. That's winter, not fall."

"Okay, I found it," Maddock said. "Max Schmeling fought an American boxer named Steve Hamas on October 3, 1935."

"That was twenty days before Dutch's death," Michelle noted.

"The fight took place in Hamburg, Germany," Maddock continued. "Max knocked Hamas out in the ninth round. Hamas had beaten Schmeling in Philadelphia the year before."

"So, Dutch was saying if Hamas had come back to the U.S., he might have beaten Schmeling again."

"That's what it appears, but I'm not understanding the relevance," Maddock said.

"Me either," Bones replied. "Why the reference to Coca-Cola and the use of the term *certified KO*? And why is this even a note in the book?"

"All good questions," Maddock said. "More coded messages I suppose—some message that might lead to his cash."

"I'm not interested in the cash," she said.

Bones and Maddock exchanged glances. "Ok, now we're really confused," Bones said.

"Allow me to explain," she said, pulling a sheaf of papers from her bag. "This is a report prepared by a friend of mine who works on Wall Street. He did some digging for me. The report shows that, in 1929, Arthur Flegenheimer bought five shares of stock in Coca-Cola for forty-dollars per share. The purchase was issued as one negotiable paper stock certificate. It was never redeemed."

"Who is Arthur Flag In Jingle Heimer Schmidt?" Bones asked.

"Flegenheimer," Michelle corrected. "That's the real name of Dutch Schultz. 'Dutch' was a nickname he picked up because he didn't think Arthur sounded very intimidating."

"He's right about that," Bones agreed.

"I'm not following you," Maddock said.

"Well, can you imagine, you're somewhere, and a guy comes running up to you while screaming, 'Oh my god! Take cover—*Arthur Flegenheimer* is here.'" Bones feigned fright.

"No, I don't mean that," Maddock scoffed. "I don't get the *stock* reference."

"I've been giving that section a lot of thought. I think the note you read was a clue," she said. "With regard to the phrases *Coke, certified, stock* and *KO*, I think it was code to let my great-grandmother know that the safe held those five shares of Coca-Cola stock, purchased in 1929. The reference to 'Coke' is obvious, but the interesting reference is to 'stock' and 'KO.' 'KO' is the stock market ticker symbol of Coca-Cola. Dutch also wrote, 'his *stock* is on the rise,' and there was also use of the term *certified*, as in 'certified stock certificate.'"

"Ok, so what?" Bones said. "Five shares of Coca-Cola, big deal."

"It *is* a big deal," she said. "One share of Coca-Cola purchased in 1929 would be worth millions today."

"Holy crap!" Bones said, perking up to full attention.

"That's a bit of a stretch, don't you think?" Maddock said. "It could have been just a boxing reference. It was well known that the Dutchman was a big boxing fan."

"Which is precisely why I believe this is a code," Michelle said. "He took my great-grandmother to a few boxing matches. I know this because she saved some of the programs as souvenirs—they were in her scrapbook."

"You may be onto something," Maddock said.

"And you think 'Certified KO' is a reference to Coca-Cola stock certificates?" Bones added.

"They were bought by the Dutchman; they were never redeemed. There may be close to fifty million dollars in Coca-Cola stock certificates in that safe. Those were purchased legally and in his name. My family is blood-related, and if you look at the note on page 132, you will note that Dutch intended for my great-grandmother to have the safe and all its contents."

Maddock turned to page 132. The scribbled note read, "*Michelle, Stay safe. All that I have is yours. Seek it out. I give you everything.*"

Maddock read the line again and sat for a moment, reflecting.

"He used the word 'safe' again," Bones said.

"I noticed," Maddock replied.

"It very much looks like he wanted your great-grandmother to find his safe and that he wanted her to have the contents," Bones said. "I think if you can prove this was written by the Dutchman himself, you'd have a strong legal claim."

"That was my conclusion as well. My great-grandmother was pregnant with my grandmother at the time. Dutch knew he wasn't going to be around. This was his way of providing for the woman he loved and her daughter—I'm certain of it."

"How do we know Dutch is the one who wrote these notes?" Bones asked.

"All the handwriting *is* the same," Michelle said, "and I have strong evidence the writing is Dutch's. I had two separate handwriting analysts compare it to known documents written by Dutch Schultz—it's identical. I have notarized written documentation from both analysts. The handwriting in this book is authentic; it will hold up in court. I'm sure of it."

Maddock began to rummage through other notes, all of which appeared cryptic. "Some of these notes seem to be totally at random with no obvious relevance. What do they mean? Take this one as an example: *Have you ever been to Chicago? I hear it's a great town. I'd love to see it one day.*"

She sighed and shook her head. "I don't know. I need your help figuring it out and, of course, to find the safe, open it, and retrieve its contents. I'm convinced that the notes lining those pages provide clues to finding its location. No one has ever had access to this information before. If you and Bones help me find the safe, I'll give you a third of everything I get to keep."

Maddock looked to Bones. "Well, what do you think?"

Bones was mentally adding up the possibilities. "I don't see why not."

"Okay, Michelle," Maddock said, "you've got a deal."

FOUR

"Bones and I will start in the morning." Maddock extended his hand to shake, but Michelle folded her arms and frowned.

"*We'll* start in the morning," she said. "I'm coming with you."

Bones shook his head. "Not a great idea. Maddock and I work better on our own."

"It's not negotiable," Michelle said, pulling the book back.

Bones and Maddock looked at each other. Maddock shrugged. Bones rolled his eyes and gave a small nod.

"Okay, then," Maddock said. "Welcome to the team. Where are you staying?"

"The Borgata," she said. "Same place as both of you."

"Then I suggest we turn in and get started first thing tomorrow," Bones said. "Want to share a taxi back to the hotel?"

Michelle nodded and smiled. She paid the bill as promised while Bones hailed a cab. "Hurry," he said to the others. "I've never found a cab this quick in Atlantic City before."

Maddock, Bones and Michelle slid into the back seat of the cab.

"Where to?" the driver asked. He was young, blonde and muscular. Maddock looked at the picture of the driver on the taxi license posted in the back seat. The picture was of an older curly-haired man of Middle Eastern descent.

"Excuse me, sir," Maddock said, "but you don't look like Mr. Kahlil Mahmood."

In one deft motion, the driver pulled a pistol, turned and pointed it at Michelle's face, his hand extending into the back seat area. "Hand over the book, now!" he demanded.

Michelle froze.

"What book?" Maddock asked.

"Don't waste time," he said. "Hand it to me. Now, or this woman dies!"

With cat-like quickness, Bones reached out, grabbed the driver's wrist and thrust it up, slamming it into the roof of the cab. The gun went off, firing a single bullet through the top of the vehicle. Maddock grabbed the man's arm, further immobilizing him, while Bones wrestled the gun out of his hands.

Disarmed, the driver wriggled free of their grasp and hastily exited the taxi, spilling out onto the street. He immediately took off running, heading east on Pop Lloyd Boulevard.

"Stay with Michelle! There might be more of them." Maddock scrambled out of the taxi and gave chase.

The milling crowd slowed his progress, and he could barely keep an eye on the back of the driver's head as it zigged and zagged through the milling crowd. The man cut through the crowd, up onto a sidewalk covered by a low overhang. Maddock tracked his movement by the people up ahead who suddenly sprang to the side.

He dodged a couple of drunken tourists, rounded a parked shuttle bus, and flashed past the entrance to Bally's. Artificial light bathed him as he moved into the covered drive that flanked the casino. Up ahead, his quarry dodged behind one of the sturdy columns topped by a decorative gold capital and adorned with an ornate letter B.

The fleeing man rounded the corner onto Park Place, headed toward the waterfront, and veered across the street. Horns blared and tires screeched as he recklessly headed into moving traffic. A few drivers took the time to stop, yell, and flash obscene gestures in the man's direction. Maddock took advantage of the pause in the traffic to dash across the street.

He was closing the gap on the driver. Up ahead, a black wrought iron fence barred the way. The man cut a sharp left and wove through the gates leading into Brighton Park.

Tourists filled the park, some holding hands, others shouting, laughing raucously, or waving drinks around. The paving stones beneath his feet were damp with humidity. The place smelled of salt air and cigarette smoke.

Up ahead, a large fountain barred the way. The fleeing driver rounded it on the right, and Maddock made to follow. Just then, a young man, smiling up at his selfie stick, took a sudden step back into Maddock's path.

"Watch out!"

Too late. Maddock plowed into the man, knocking him to the side, and stumbled. A sharp pain erupted in his shins as he struck something sold. Next thing he knew, he lurched forward. Cold water enveloped him for a split second and then he cracked his head hard enough that he saw stars.

He had fallen into the fountain.

Head ringing, he clambered to his feet, sloshed to the fountain wall, and heaved himself over the side.

"Hey jerk, you ran me over!" The young man froze, eyes wide, when he saw the look in Maddock's eyes.

"Sorry," Maddock grunted before turning and

resuming the pursuit. His head wasn't quite clear and he jogged forward, shoes squishing, water streaming down his body. People stared as he passed.

At the end of the park, he froze. For a brief, irrational moment he believed he had come face to face with a group of armed men. And then his muddled brain began to piece together his surroundings.

An impossibly tall man stood before him, head hung low, looking down at a pair of dog tags in his hand. Behind him, a group of soldiers approached, carrying a wounded comrade. They were flying. No, they were mounted on a wall. Not soldiers…sculptures. The tall man was a statue.

His eyes drifted to the left, where a golden sculpture of a torch topped a smooth black wall engraved with the words NEW JERSEY KOREAN WAR MEMORIAL. Beneath it were the names of the fallen.

"Of course," he muttered. "I saw this earlier today."

"Sir, are you all right?" A petite young woman with short hair and brown eyes and skin looked up at him with concern. "Your head is bleeding."

"I…I took a spill back there."

"You might have a concussion," she said.

"Yeah. Did you see a man running away?" He tried to describe the cab driver, but found he couldn't picture the man's face.

"Where are you staying?" the girl asked. "I'll walk you back."

"It's all right. My friends are back at the oyster bar." Turning away, he stumbled back through the park.

Bones and Michelle met him on the other side of the park. It was a measure of Bones' anger that he didn't laugh at Maddock for his tumble into the fountain.

"What's the deal, Michelle?" Bones said. "You lied to us. You said no one else knew about the book."

"I didn't lie," she insisted. "I said no one has ever *seen* the book, except my family. I didn't say that no one knew about it."

"A lie of omission is still a lie," Maddock said, rubbing the bump swelling on his head. "And you put us in danger by withholding that information."

"I can explain." She looked around nervously. "Let's get out of here before the authorities arrive. I don't want to have this conversation with them. Let's get back to the Borgata, get Maddock cleaned up, and get our stuff. If they found me here, they now know you are with me. It's not safe for any of us now. Let's move to a different hotel I'll explain it all to you."

FIVE

Two hours later the three of them sat in the 24-hour café of the Golden Nugget. Michelle had donned a New York Mets baseball cap and pulled her hair back in a ponytail. She also wore a pair of non-prescription glasses. Maddock had to admit he liked the look. All around them were bleary-eyed patrons sipping coffee and, by the sad looks on their faces, nursing regrets. Probably licking their wounds after a hard night at the tables or the slots.

"How's your head?" Bones asked. "I mean, compared to usual."

"It's all right," Maddock lied. Sharp pain still pierced his frontal lobe. "I don't think I have a concussion."

"Did you know Jackie Chan got a concussion and a broken nose filming his own stunts?" Michelle piped up.

Bones and Maddock turned slowly to stare at her.

"What?" Bones asked.

"Sorry. I have a lot of random facts in my head. I tend to spout them at odd times."

"Never mind that," Maddock said, turning back toward Bones. "Do you think we were followed?" Maddock asked.

"No, I don't think so," Bones replied.

"Are you sure?"

He shook his head. "Never one hundred percent sure. What about the hotel check-in? If these people are connected, maybe they can trace the card."

"I called Kaylin and got her to make our reservations through her own card," Michelle said. "I'll pay her back. There's no way anyone knows her connection or I'd be dead by now. You two are sharing a room under the name Bill and Sam Smith, by the way."

"Very creative," Bones replied. "We don't look like brothers so I guess that means we're hitched?"

"If that's how you want to see it."

"Well, there's obviously a third party who knows about the book," Maddock said. "That guy came at us with bad intentions."

"That was crazy," Michelle said. "What a rush! I've never had a gun pointed at my head before. Beats the hell out of skydiving."

"It gets old after a while," Bones said. "Trust me."

"Okay, tell us what all that was about," Maddock demanded. "What have you gotten us into here?"

She hesitated, took a deep breath, and gazed out into the casino area, as if looking for signs they were being watched. Seemingly satisfied, she spoke.

"My mother gave me that book when I was a little girl. It had been handed down from my great-grandmother. My mother never told me there was any connection to Dutch Schultz until very recently. For all practical purposes, I grew up thinking it was just an old book that had been handed down to my mother. I'd seen the notes before, but without the context. It all looked like gibberish to me, and I never gave them a second thought. That all changed three months ago."

"What happened three months ago?" Maddock asked.

"My mother lived in Newark," she said. "About three months ago three men showed up at my mother's door, unannounced—out of the blue. They flashed a badge and said they were with the FBI and were investigating an old case involving a missing book, a first edition copy of

Mary Poppins."

"Does the book itself have value?" Maddock asked.

"Yes, it does," Michelle replied. "A first edition of Mary Poppins in good condition is worth between $2,000 to $3,000 to a collector. My mother and I had it appraised a couple of times over the years."

"Go on," Bones said.

"My mother was savvy enough to realize that a $3,000 book from 1934 would not warrant an entire investigation from the FBI so many years later," she said. "She also said the men didn't look like FBI agents and that the man with the badge flashed it so quickly she became suspicious."

"What did she do?" Bones asked.

"She made up a story on the spot that the book had been sold in a yard sale more than ten years ago. She thought the story satisfied the men because they thanked her and left. She called me right away to tell me all about it—the experience spooked her. We both wondered how anyone could have traced the book to her after all these years—it didn't make sense. That's when she dropped the bomb on me that my great-grandfather was none other than the notorious Dutch Schultz."

"That was the *very first time* you realized you were related to Shultz?" Bones confirmed.

"Yes," she said.

"What happened next?" Maddock asked. "Did you call the FBI?"

"Not at that time," Michelle said. "I wanted to. I urged her to, but at the time, she was not certain the men were imposters. She still thought there was a chance they were real FBI agents."

"Go on," Bones said.

"That's when we started looking more closely at the notes written in the margins by Dutch," Michelle said. "My mother had seen them many times. She always thought it was random gibberish, as did her mother before her. I began to Google all the verbiage in the notes. Finally, I Googled '*Devil*,' '*Face*,' and '*Dutch Schultz*.' That's when I turned up all the information on the treasure hidden prior to his death."

"I'll bet that freaked you out," Bones said, "to discover all this new information after all these years."

"It did, but the story doesn't end there," she replied. "Two days later my mother's house was broken into and ransacked." She paused, bit her lower lip. When she spoke again, her voice was thick with emotion. "They killed her." Tears welled in her eyes and her gaze dropped to her hands.

Maddock put his hand on her shoulder. "Michelle, I'm so sorry."

She managed a weak "thank you." She dabbed her eyes and drank from her water glass before continuing. "The police took me to the station and began to question me about what I knew about the three men, what they were looking for and why they would want to harm my mother."

"What did you tell them?" Bones asked.

"I told them exactly what happened; three men showed up at the house and identified themselves as FBI agents, and said they were investigating an old case," she said.

"And did the police call the FBI?"

"They did. The FBI claimed they were not involved."

"And you didn't mention the book at all?" Maddock said.

"No. I didn't know who to trust," she said. "After I was questioned by the FBI, they released me. When I got home, I found that my own house had also been searched. They had virtually destroyed my home looking for that book. If I hadn't been questioned by the FBI at that very time, I'm certain I would have been tortured for information and killed."

"And obviously, they didn't find the book," Maddock noted, holding it up.

"I had it stored in a safety deposit box at the bank," she said. "At the time, I didn't know exactly what I had but I did know it was a first edition of *Mary Poppins* worth about $3,000. I also knew there were people out there willing to kill for it, and obviously not for the value of the book itself. I decided then and there I was going to uncover the story behind it."

"What did you do next?"

"I went to the bank and withdrew all my savings in cash, everything I had, about $21,000. And I got the book. That's when I remembered that Kaylin had once told me about the adventures the three of you had shared. My connection to her was loose enough that anyone looking for me would not think to find me with her. She took me in. I left everything behind and stayed with her. She helped me. We began researching Dutch Schultz together. We read one article that claimed Dutch had bought Liberty Bonds at one time. That's when I began to investigate his dealings in the stock market and that's how I uncovered the information about his Coca-Cola stock. Once we started looking at all of Dutch's notes, it became more and more obvious that the book was a map of sorts, one that might lead me to where his safe was buried."

"And naturally, you reached out to us to solve your mystery," Bones said.

"Well, Nicolas Cage wasn't available." She managed a tight smile.

"Who are these people?" Maddock asked. "The ones trying to obtain the book?"

"And after all these years, how did they know how your mother had it?" Bones added.

"And why now?" Maddock concluded. "Why not ten years ago, or twenty years ago?"

"All good questions," Michelle asked. "If I knew the answers to any of them I'd tell you, but I don't."

"So, what now?" Bones asked.

"What do you mean, what now?" Michelle asked.

"I mean, it's a whole different kettle of fish," Bones replied.

"How so?" she said.

"I don't know, let's think. We're not one hundred percent sure if there's really a safe to find, and if there is, it may or may not contain cash, or Liberty bonds, or gold coins, and may or may not have Coca-Cola certificates in it. If the cash is there, the government will probably seize it. If the certificates are there, they may or may not be redeemable, and if they are redeemable, you may or may not be entitled to them. We have an unknown enemy of unknown size, with unknown resources, who will kill us for the book and might even be watching us eat at this very moment. And the only thing we have to go on is Mary freaking Poppins."

Michelle's eyes widened and her face trembled with a mixture of anger and confusion. "Well," she finally, said "when you put it like that, it sounds a bit complicated, doesn't it?" She turned to Maddock. "What do *you* think, Dane?"

"I think we should check it out," he replied.

Bones thought for a moment, then shrugged. "Me too."

SIX

Bones let his eyes wander, taking in the scenery from his seat on the Amtrak leaving Atlantic City. He glanced over at Maddock. For the last hour his friend had been studying the notes written in the margins of *Mary Poppins* by Dutch Schultz.

"Tell me again why we're taking the train?" Michelle asked from the seat next to Maddock. "It won't even get us to Phoenicia. Why not just hop on a puddle jumper?"

"Because whoever is tailing us will most likely be looking for us at the airport," Maddock said. "If we were being watched, they'll expect us to take a cab to the airport or leave the hotel in our own car. Doing it this way makes it far less likely we'll be followed. And since there's no train station in Phoenicia," he continued, "we're going to get off at the nearest station in Kingston and rent a car and drive the rest of the way to the Devil's Face formation. It's only about a forty-five-minute drive."

"Did you know air travel is statistically safer than trains?" Michelle asked.

Bones shook his head. "Chick, you have got to cut that out."

"I'll try, but no promises."

"I don't like the way this hunt is shaping up," Bones said. "I hate burner phones. I really dislike looking for treasure knowing someone is looking for us."

"We've been in that situation before," Maddock said. "We don't know anything about the people who are trying to secure our map—"

"You mean, our *book!*" Bones said.

"Yes, a book. At this point, if the people looking for us found out about the book and its location after all this time, you have to assume they are well-organized and well-financed. You also have to assume the FBI is on to this, too. It would not take very many steps for them to connect all this to Dutch Schultz's safe. I would expect to see someone show up from the FBI sooner rather than later. The tough part is going to be deciphering the information and finding the safe before the FBI and this other interested third party finds us. Hopefully, Jimmy can narrow our search parameters a bit."

"Jimmy?" asked Michelle.

"Jimmy Letson. An old buddy of ours. He's a writer for the *Washington Post*. He's also an I.T. whiz kid."

"And by that, he means a hacker," Bones said.

Maddock ignored him. "He's not an official part of our team, but he's great at finding information and he's a real enthusiast for the kind of work we do. I asked him to get me everything he could find on Dutch Schultz and every documented treasure hunt for The Dutchman's safe."

"But no one's found anything," she said.

"That's right, but there have been lots of attempts," Maddock replied. "It will save us a lot of time knowing where *not* to look."

"It would also help if we could find out who is on your trail and how they found out about the book after all these years," Bones added.

"I'll add that to the list of things for Jimmy to ferret out," Maddock said. "You said that the book was given to your great-grandmother's brother, a man named Alex Singer, the night Dutch was murdered, correct?"

"Yes, what does that have to do with anything?" she

asked.

He shrugged, "Maybe nothing, but you never know. I asked Jimmy to look into Alex Singer as well."

"You've been looking at that book since this morning," Bones said. "Have you come up with anything?"

"I think we'll start at the Devil's Face formation and see where it leads from there," Maddock said. "It's widely held by treasure hunting enthusiasts as the final resting place of that safe. The book has a number of references to it as well."

He flipped through the pages of the book. "Here's one on page seventy-eight. It reads, *See what the devil sees.* Here is another on page eighty, *The Devil has the answers.* On page ninety it says, *Remember, the devil is a trickster.* On page ninety-four it says, *The devil can't see the forest for the trees.*"

"How can anyone make anything from that gibberish?" Bones asked.

"It's possible that the Dutchman thought Michelle's great-grandmother would understand it all. The code was probably a precaution in the event the book fell into someone else's hands."

Bones looked at Michelle. "If all that's true, how come your great-granny didn't find the safe?"

"She was pregnant with my grandmother at the time of Dutch Schultz's death," Michelle said. "She had a problem pregnancy. She was in the hospital for weeks. She was broke and an unwed mother—I can't imagine what life must have been like. Try to imagine a single mom with no money in 1935 skipping across the country in search of treasure."

"All good points," Bones said.

"We'll be in Kingston in about fifteen minutes," Maddock said. "The rock formation is near Stoney Clove Creek. We'll rent a car and be at Devil's Face before noon."

SEVEN

The Devil's Face formation was an incredible geological wonder, in Maddock's estimation. The formation was off the main road, about a hundred and fifty yards up a fairly steep incline that was heavily covered in trees and thick bush.

Maddock had to admit, the formation looked very much like a face, albeit an evil-looking one—creepy by anyone's standards. Broad forehead, eyes shrouded in shadow, mouth a deep gash. He could certainly understand how the rock formation got its name.

Jimmy Letson had emailed him a couple dozen pages of information that he had dug up pertaining to previous attempts to find Dutch's treasure, and he had reviewed the information during their drive from Kingston. The Devil's Face formation, along with a large boulder at the outskirts of Phoenicia known as the Devil's Tombstone, served as fodder for dozens of Devil sightings, many of which had been etched into local folklore.

One of those stories involved the Devil leaving his mark on a sheet of paper, including the locations of the Devil's Face and the Devil's Tombstone. This led to much speculation about the treasure of Dutch Schultz, who was a murderer and mobster and to some folks' way of thinking, had gone to meet the devil when he died.

That led to massive searches and excavations by thousands of amateur and professional treasure hunters, all of which turned up nothing.

"According to Jimmy's notes, the most popular theory by far is that Dutch buried the money in a steel safe or suitcase under, near or adjacent to the Devil's

Face. Every inch of the ground all around the formation has been dug up and scanned by metal detectors."

"And nothing's been found?" Bones asked. "No clues? No leads?"

"Nothing," Maddock replied.

"Why are we even here?" Bones asked.

"Because there are a dozen references to Devil's Face in Dutch's notes," Maddock replied. "This formation plays some role in the whereabouts of the safe. We don't know what it is yet. We have to figure it out."

"Dutch wrote a note about what the devil sees, right?" Michelle said.

"*See what the devil sees*," Maddock quoted. "The formation is facing what direction?"

Bones looked at the formation carefully. "South," he said. "Actually, more southeast."

"And when we look southeast ..." Maddock began.

Michelle looked off in the direction that the formation faced. "All I see are trees."

"Do you think he may have buried the money along the sightline of how the formation faces?" Bones asked.

"That was yet another theory," Maddock replied.

"So, that whole area has been searched and dug up too?"

"Jimmy's notes have the entire area southeast of here being scanned with metal detectors and dug up."

"What about ground penetrating radar?" Bones asked.

"According to his notes, there were at least two archaeological expeditions where ground-penetrating radar was used over this entire area," Maddock said. "It revealed nothing."

"What the hell is ground penetrating radar?"

Michelle asked.

"Just what it sounds like," Maddock said. "It's radar imaging used to find objects under the earth. Archaeologists commonly use it to find relics and dinosaur bones."

"Criminologists use it to find human remains," Bones added.

"Another note says, '*The Devil can't see the forest for the trees*,'" Michelle added. "What do you think that means?"

"Not sure," Maddock replied. "Let's make our way up to the formation and see if we can pick up anything new."

Bones turned to Michelle. "Are you up for a hike? You can hang back if you want."

"You mean because I'm a girl?"

"No, I just noticed you were limping a bit."

"I injured it in the service but it doesn't slow me down. I was a patriot missile crew member. That was before college, of course." She smiled at the stunned looks on the men's faces. "I'll take the lead, gentlemen," she said. "Don't fall behind."

Bones made eye contact with Maddock and rolled his eyes, smiling, as Michelle took off up the hill. The two men followed.

About two hundred yards away, a man with high-powered binoculars watched carefully from a car parked on the side of the road. He was in his early forties with prematurely graying hair. He covered it in a floppy gray safari hat. He wore a khaki vest with camo shorts and hiking shoes. He went by the code name 'Birdwatcher,' which also served as his cover story. His high-powered sniper rifle was in the trunk of his car, and his pistol was in a kidney holster, well hidden by the vest, but within easy reach should the situation call for it.

Birdwatcher was a hired assassin, and very good at what he did. He had been a sniper for the French Foreign Legion, 2nd Régiment Etranger Infanterie, or REI for short. He had thirty-six documented kills in his eight years with the REI, more than twice that number off the books. Since he left the service he'd lost track of the number of kills he'd made that were privately contracted.

After five minutes, Birdwatcher lost visual contact with his targets as they disappeared into the trees and thick foliage. He sat his binoculars on the passenger seat of the car and casually opened a Payday candy bar. As a general rule, Birdwatcher hated anything remotely associated with America. Payday candy bars were an exception to that rule—he always had plenty of them on hand.

When he found out that Dane Maddock was involved in the assignment, he jumped on the opportunity immediately.

He had crossed paths with Maddock once before. It was many years earlier, when they were both in the military. It was not a pleasant meeting. It had to do with one of Birdwatcher's clandestine missions, a kill that was not officially sanctioned. He was charged with taking out a family member of an enemy general. Maddock was part of a Navy SEAL team deployed in Africa on a joint mission with Birdwatcher's sniper squad. The mission changed in the final hour and Maddock objected to the new target, an innocent teenager, the son of the original target. Birdwatcher followed orders, however, and eagerly so. Maddock was furious after the job was completed. The pompous Navy SEAL had found him and punched him square in the jaw, knocking him out cold, in front of the more than twenty men in his squad.

He had been humiliated. If there had been any way he could have killed Maddock then and there without retribution he would have done it. For a full year following the incident Birdwatcher thought of little else but revenge. Over time the fire in his belly quelled to a glowing ember but it never completely died.

And now, after all these years, they once again shared the same space. The mere mention of his name stoked the fire again, and it was now fully ablaze.

After all this time, he would finally find justice. He smiled at the thought.

He picked up his cell phone and dialed, taking a hefty bite of the peanut caramel Payday bar. He would earn a hefty fee to complete this job, but he didn't care about the money. He would have done this job for free.

The man who had hired him answered on the third ring. His name was Antonio Rossi, but he was better known as *Virtuoso*.

"They are at Devil's Face," Birdwatcher said, in perfectly articulated English with a deep French accent. "They are scaling the hill to the formation now."

"The safe is not at Devil's Face," came the gravelly voiced reply.

"I know that."

"Then why are they there?"

"Perhaps they don't know it yet," Birdwatcher replied. "It's possible they have not unraveled whatever clues were left behind in the book."

"Have you seen the book, yet?" Virtuoso asked.

"Not yet," Birdwatcher replied. "Why don't you let

me make this easy? We know the book is with them. I can take all three of them out and bring the book to you tonight."

"No," Virtuoso said. "I did some research on Dane Maddock. He's good, perhaps even the best at what he does. We stick with the original plan—let him do the work for us. Keep a close eye on him but stay out of sight."

"You know this would have been much easier if you hadn't hired that amateur in Atlantic City. He blew it in the taxi cab. If it weren't for him they would have no idea other interested parties were following them."

"You're right," Virtuoso said. "I won't make that mistake again. Do they know you are following?"

"No."

"How can you be sure?"

"I know how people act when they think they are being watched," Birdwatcher said. "They went to great trouble finding a new hotel, using another's credit card, and taking the train rather than a plane. They think they are home free—I'm certain of it."

"*Très bon.* That's why I hired you," Virtuoso said.

"I know how to do my job," Birdwatcher replied.

Virtuoso ended the call. Birdwatch sat, seething, reflecting on how pleasant it would be to exact revenge on Maddock and end his relationship with the mobster.

"The Devil's Face," he sneered. "Just wait until you come face to face with me again, Dane Maddock. Then you'll really see the face of the devil."

EIGHT

Michelle charged up the steep incline like a mountain goat. Although they were no longer SEALs, Maddock and Bones were in excellent shape and matched her stride for stride, but even so, Maddock was breathing heavily when he and Michelle reached the formation. They paused, waiting for Bones who had pulled out his compass and was looking off in the direction the formation faced from his elevated position.

"Where's the fire?" Maddock asked, taking a sip of water. "You have something to prove?"

Michelle pulled a water bottle out of her backpack. "What? Having trouble keeping up with a girl?"

"Hey, Bones is the one who..."

"He's an odd guy," Michelle interrupted. "Odd, but interesting. Is he married, your friend?"

Maddock laughed. "Not a chance."

"Hmmm...girlfriend?"

"Not him. He's a bit of a character. A little on the high-maintenance side for most women but he's the most loyal friend I've ever known. You know, you two..."

"Say what now?" Bones asked, joining them. His hair, face and shirt were moist with sweat. His shirt was unbuttoned to his navel.

"We were just talking about you," Michelle said.

"Oh really? Was it about my wit and charm?"

"No," Michelle replied. "Maddock was just telling me that you were difficult and high maintenance."

Bones scowled. "Oh, did he now?"

"What do you want me to do? Lie?" Maddock asked.

"Screw you, Maddock."

"Let's climb to the top of the formation, shall we?" Michelle said.

"By all means, your majesty," Bones answered, offering an overplayed bow and a wave of his hand, admonishing her to lead the way.

Five minutes later, they stood at the top of Devil's Face looking in the same direction the formation faced.

"From the clues left in the book, my guess is the Devil's Face formation plays a major role in discovering the whereabouts of Dutch's treasure," Maddock said. "I'm just not so sure it's actually buried *here*. There are numerous notes about the Devil's Face and what the devil sees. So, what does the Devil see?"

Bones held up his compass. "The Devil's Face formation faces southeast. If those trees weren't blocking the view, we'd see the town of Phoenicia from here."

"There is a lot of conflicting information about what happened," Michelle said. "The most popular, perhaps best-accepted theory is that, the day before his death, Dutch and Lulu were heading north through the Catskills. They stopped for lunch at the Phoenicia Hotel and then proceeded along Route 214 to Stoney Clove Creek, arrived at the Devil's Face formation, buried the money and then headed back to Phoenicia before driving to Newark."

"That's crazy," Bones said. "They have millions of dollars in cash and perhaps negotiables hidden in a safe *in their car*? So, they casually stop for lunch at a hotel. What's wrong with this picture?"

"Maybe it was all misdirection," Michelle said. "Or maybe he thought he was being followed."

"Over the years, the details probably changed as the story was retold," Maddock said.

"It does seem odd," Bones said. "Presumably, they would have had the safe with them, maybe in the trunk of the car, right? So, they leave all that money in the car and go inside for lunch? That doesn't make sense, but then again, Dutch had a lot of heat on him. He didn't know who he could trust. Maybe he wasn't thinking clearly."

Maddock shrugged. "He was thinking clearly enough to hide his treasure where no one could find it for more than eighty years."

Michelle pulled a notebook from her backpack and began leafing through it. "After Dutch was shot, everything he said was documented," she said. "It's hard to tell if he was delirious and talking out of his head or if he was providing clues. Some of the things he said were nonsensical."

"Like what?" Bones asked.

"Like, '*You can play jacks and girls do that with a softball,*'" she said, reading from her notebook. "That's one example."

"I see what you mean. That's sort of a bat-shit crazy thing to say, isn't it?"

"But he also said, '*Lulu, drive me back to Phoenicia,*'" Michelle added. "That triggered a lot of people to believe that he wanted to go back to Phoenicia for something very precious to him."

"Like a safe full of money, coins, bonds and stock certificates, perhaps," Maddock suggested.

"And in the book, one of Dutch's notes says, '*See what the devil sees.*'" Michelle said. "The devil formation is facing Phoenicia."

"You can't see Phoenicia from here," Bones said. "The trees block the view."

"One of the notes also said, '*The devil is a trickster*,' which could be a clue or misdirection," Maddock noted. "Phoenicia has also been turned inside out by treasure hunters."

"Still, it's worth a look," Michelle said. "The formation definitely faces Phoenicia."

"I agree," Maddock said. "Bones, use your phone to mark our exact location. I doubt Dutch had the technology in those days to follow a direct path from the eyes of the formation, but when we get to Phoenicia I'd like to follow his relative line of sight and see what we find. Let's go."

NINE

Maddock, Bones and Michelle made their way back to the rental car which was parked on the main highway.

"How far is Phoenicia from here?" Michelle asked.

"What? That's not one of your random facts?" Bones asked.

"Go to hell."

"It's just a few minutes by car," Maddock said. "We can start at the hotel where Dutch and Lulu Rosencrantz were said to have had lunch."

"And we should probably just check in, too, don't you think?" Michelle said. "That's where our reservations are."

Maddock sighed. "I didn't even think about making reservations."

"I did," Michelle said, "but unfortunately there were only two rooms available."

"I don't mind sharing with Michelle," Bones piped in.

Michelle rolled her eyes. "In your dreams, Geronimo."

"Oh, c'mon now," he protested. "Don't you want to see my war dance?"

"No," she said, "and I don't want to think about your peace pipe, either."

Maddock chuckled.

"You're no fun," Bones retorted.

At the Phoenicia Hotel, Maddock met the manager, a man named Quigley. He had worked there since 1992 and prided himself as somewhat of an expert on Dutch

Shultz folklore. He knew precisely where Dutch and Lulu had lunch and showed them where legend had it that they had parked their car.

"You're certain that they ate lunch at this table," Maddock reiterated.

"As certain as I can be," Quigley replied. "The information was passed down as a legend, and that part seems certain. There were a number of witnesses—employees who saw them together at the time. Less reliable is the information as to where they parked their car. There are several different accounts."

"I don't think it really matters," Maddock said. "From this table, there is no clear view of the parking lot. Dutch was paranoid. I seriously doubt he'd leave a safe filled with several million dollars in cash, coins and negotiables in a car and not have it in his line of sight."

"Yeah, that makes sense," Bones said. "And really, unless this dining room has been remodeled, there is really no place else they could have sat and seen a car parked in the lot."

"There have been renovations," Quigley said, "but no major design updates. The dining room today, is very similar to what Mr. Schultz would have seen in 1935."

"Mr. Quigley, one of the rumors about that day was that Dutch and Lulu Rosencrantz stayed here the night before," Michelle said. "Do you know one way or the other?"

"I can tell you they are not on our books," Quigley responded. "It's possible they stayed under an assumed name, but we have no record of two men staying together in a single room for that night and no record of two men staying in adjoining rooms. The vacancy rate for that evening was high. Something would have stood out."

"Isn't it possible that Dutch slipped the clerk a fifty dollar bill to keep all names off the books?" Bones asked.

"Yes, certainly," Quigley said. He paused a beat, then continued. "Over time every inch of this hotel and our grounds have been combed for potential places they might have hidden the treasure. I have taken part in many of those searches myself."

"You came up with nothing even remotely suspicious?" Maddock asked.

Quigley shook his head. "I'm convinced they didn't stay here. I think they stopped off for lunch on their way to Newark, but to be honest, I'm skeptical there was a safe in their car. As you said, Mr. Maddock, it would be hard to imagine them coming in here for a casual lunch and leaving a safe filled with money by itself in the parking lot."

"Did any folklore mention whether or not their clothes were dirty or muddy?" Maddock said.

"No, why?"

"Well, if they had buried the treasure prior to having lunch they would have probably been dirty."

"Never heard anything like that," Quigley said.

"Thank you for your time, Mr. Quigley," Maddock said. "Do you mind if we snoop around the grounds a bit?"

"Please, by all means," he said.

Outside, Maddock asked Bones for the GPS coordinates to Devil's Face. Once he retrieved them he looked in the direction of the rock formation.

"The money is not at the hotel," he said.

"What makes you say that?" Michelle asked.

"*See what the Devil sees*," he quoted. "The hotel is on

the far west side of Phoenicia. The view of the formation is blocked by the hillside. Even if there were no trees at that time, Dutch would not be able to see the formation from here, nor would he be able to see the hotel from the formation."

Bones scratched his chin. "Well, that's one possibility we've ruled out. Now what?"

"We start investigating all the other clues, one by one," he said. "I vote we turn in early and get an early start in the morning."

TEN

The Phoenicia Library was located on Main Street in between an imports store and a delicatessen. The tiny two-story building had once been someone's home. A simple sign reading PHOENICIA LIBRARY hung over the window at the library's front. To its right was a bulletin board of community events. To the left, a white door with the street number 48 above it opened into the library.

The tiny hamlet of Phoenicia appealed to Maddock. Nestled in the Catskills, it had a simple charm. The sea would always be his first love, but he enjoyed the mountains, too.

"Shouldn't take too long to check this place out," Bones said. "I think Maddock has more books on the back of his toilet than this place holds." He paused, frowned thoughtfully. "Wait a minute, those aren't books. Those are Playboys."

"Phoenicia isn't exactly a large town," Michelle said. "In the last census, its population was only three hundred and nine."

"What did I tell you about spouting trivia?"

"I'll spout whatever I want."

Bones grinned. "That's what she said."

"Don't even start."

Maddock heaved a deep sigh. He couldn't tell if Bones and Michelle attracted or annoyed one another. Maybe it was a bit of both.

"Michelle and I will check out the local history section. Bones, you do what you do best."

"What's that? Hook up with the librarian?"

"Wander aimlessly and try to stumble onto something unexpected."

"Can do." With that, Bones turned on his heel and walked away.

The interior of the library was bright and airy, with white walls, and wooden floors polished to a high sheen. Maddock and Michelle quickly identified the appropriate section and began flipping through the few books. It wasn't long before Maddock noticed something odd.

A man, heavyset with broad shoulders and a florid face, was standing nearby, trying and failing to appear inconspicuous. Out of the corner of his eye, Maddock watched as the fellow peered over the top of a *Field & Stream* magazine, watching him with narrow eyed intensity. When Maddock turned toward him, the man raised his magazine again.

"Amateur," Maddock scoffed in a scant whisper.

"What's that?" Michelle asked.

"I'll tell you in a minute. Let's make a move. Just play along."

They headed over to the Geography section and made a show of examining a book about the Catskills. Sure enough, the man followed.

"Whatever I say or do, just nod and follow along," Maddock whispered. "Trust me."

Michelle nodded to show she agreed.

Maddock tapped a page. "I think this is what we're looking for," he said in a conversational tone, loud enough to carry. "Read it and see what you think. I'm going to look something up."

As Michelle pretended to read, he took out his phone and tapped out a message to Bones.

Someone's following us. We're going to leave. Hang back long enough to see if he follows.

Bones replied with a thumbs up.

"I think you're right," Michelle said.

"It's just down the street from here. Let's go."

They exited the library and made a left on Main Street. They strolled along, Maddock trying to convey a sense of purpose as he walked. They passed a liquor store, a real estate agency, and a fine arts gallery, then headed out onto the bridge that spanned the swiftly moving waters of Stoney Clove Creek. When they reached the other side, he paused and stole a casual glance back.

The man was still following them, and as Maddock turned, he froze, turned away, and pretended to check his cell phone.

"Now." Maddock grabbed Michelle by the arm and they ducked behind an overgrown hedge. "Stay back. Let me deal with this."

Michelle frowned, but agreed. She moved deeper into the dense patch of greenery and disappeared from sight.

Maddock ducked down and tensed to spring. He caught a glimpse of movement, watched as the figure came closer. Over the low rush of the creek, he heard the man let out a surprised grunt. Quick footsteps, and then Maddock sprang his trap.

The man had been expecting it. He leaped to the side and swung a meaty fist at Maddock's head. The blow missed and Maddock countered with a stiff uppercut to the chin and a roundhouse kick that just missed the man's kidney. It landed hard, though, and the man let out a grunt of pain.

Hopefully I cracked his ribs.

The fellow was resilient and didn't give up so easily. He threw a wild haymaker that, if it had landed, would have turned Maddock's lights out. Maddock ducked the blow, landed two sharp jabs that sent blood flowing from his stalker's nose, and then dug a heavy punch into the man's injured ribs.

The man staggered back in the direction of the bridge and dropped to one knee.

"Who the hell are you and why are you following us?"

The man gritted his teeth, drew a knife from inside his boot, and attacked.

Like so many amateurs, the fellow was clueless about knife fighting. He raised the knife high overhead as he charged.

Moving fast, Maddock leaped in, seized him by the wrist, and then head-butted him across the bridge of the nose.

The man let out a curse, let go of his knife, and took a step back. Maddock caught him with a right cross to the jaw that turned his legs to rubber.

"Nice job, Maddock. You made him do the stanky leg." Bones had caught up to them. He quickly pinned the man's arm behind his back. "Holy crap, it's the cowboy."

"Who?" Maddock asked.

"He was at the casino. He's even worse at Texas Hold 'Em than I am."

"What does he want?" Michelle had emerged from her hiding place.

"Same thing the cab driver wanted. To kill us."

"No," the man called cowboy grunted. "Heard the

two of you talking. Knew something was up. Got curious."

"Are you trying to tell me you've been following us all this time?" Maddock didn't buy it. The man was no good at sneaking.

"I was at the oyster bar. Heard enough to start doing some investigating of my own. Saw you in the library and followed you."

"Here's the deal," Bones said. "You're going to stop following us, and you're going to get the hell out of Phoenicia and go back to whatever inbreeder cesspit you crawled out of. You hear me?"

"I've got as much right as you to look for the treasure."

"Sure you do," Maddock said. "But if I were you, I'd find a new mystery to solve. Let him go, Bones."

Bones release his grip on the cowboy, but as soon as he did, the man turned and threw a punch that just missed.

"Big mistake, asshat." With surprising quickness for a man of his size, Bones drove the heel of his palm into the cowboy's nose, then spun him around. He grabbed the stunned man and lifted him off the ground.

"What are you doing?" the man snarled, his fists beating uselessly on Bones' back.

"We're going to wash that blood off of you." Bones took three steps out onto the bridge and dumped the screaming man over the side.

"Well," he said, turning back to Maddock and Michelle. "That ought to cool him off."

Birdwatcher slowly made his way down to the edge of the creek, careful to remain behind cover. The man

Bonebrake had pitched into the water was down on his hands and knees, spewing a stream of epithets and vowing revenge on the big Indian. Checking to make sure no one was looking, he stepped out into the open.

"Let me give you a hand."

Surprise and confusion filled the man's eyes as he gazed up at this unexpected arrival.

"Who the hell are you?"

"A friend." Birdwatcher paused. "Well, I'm the enemy of your enemy. Perhaps we can help each other."

Wordlessly, the man permitted Birdwatcher to haul him out of the water.

"We need to talk. Out of sight." Birdwatcher led him back along the creek bank, away from town and from prying eyes.

When he was satisfied that they were well away, he turned.

"You're going to help me get back at that Indian?"

"I'm going to make sure you are never bothered by him again."

The man's eyes went wide with shock as the stiletto plunged into his heart. His lips moved, but no sound came out.

"Please understand, this is nothing personal, but I can't have you interfering with the hunt. And my orders are not to kill Maddock and Bonebrake. My employer said nothing about buffoons who blunder into my path."

He took a step back and the man fell limply to the ground. Birdwatcher wiped his blade on the man's shirt then took a minute to cover him over with leaves and brush. He had a feeling it would be a long time before anyone found the body. In any case, they had no reason to connect him with the killing.

He stood, took in a deep, refreshing breath of crisp mountain air, and smiled.

"Back to work."

ELEVEN

Over the next few days, Maddock, Bones and Michelle poured over the notes the Dutchman had written in the first edition of *Mary Poppins*. They dissected every word, every possible connotation.

They cross-referenced every handwritten note with documentation left by other treasure seekers.

They found and interviewed long-time residents, people in their eighties and nineties who were still of sharp mind. Outside of the Devil's Face formation, many fortune hunters had focused on landmarks along the nearby Esopus River. Though the banks of the river had been thoroughly scoured, they spent two entire days driving parallel to the river and walking its banks.

Maddock paid special attention to parts of the river that would be visible from the Devil's Face formation.

Their investigation turned up nothing.

By the end of their sixth day, they had covered every inch of Phoenicia and the territory leading from there to the rock formation. Bones was the first to express his frustration and dismay. Maddock was feeling much the same but held it in. Neither of them knew what Michelle was thinking.

It was obvious to all of them, however, that they were out of new ideas and the search was a dead end. The only positive was that the cowboy seemed to have disappeared. He must have taken their warning to heart.

The only thing that qualified as eventful was a spark of romance between Bones and Michelle, one that had burned brightly for a moment but quickly fizzled. They'd enjoyed drinks together, and a little extra, the first few nights. But after several days of fruitless searching, the tension and frustration got in the way. Michelle retreated to her room after each day's searching was completed. No drinks, not even dinner with Bones and Maddock. Bones and Michelle began to snap at each other during the course of the day. Even though there had been an initial attraction, it was obvious that the two of them irritated each other. Maddock found himself thrust into the role of referee, which began to grate on his nerves as well.

Just after noon on day seven of the search, Maddock, Bones and Michelle sat quietly at a window table at the Phoenicia Diner, on Route 28. The original owners had opened the diner in 1962, and it remained a family restaurant for 30 years, moving to its present location in the early 1980s. The current owner worked hard to maintain the diner's traditional feel. The menu included sandwiches, a few entrees, soup, salad, and all-day breakfast. The décor was classic diner: bright and airy with lots of faux-wood, cozy booths, and a bar that ran the length of the restaurant. The large windows provided a breathtaking view of the Catskills.

"This place definitely has the classic diner vibe," Maddock said as they stepped inside.

"Yeah, except for all the hipsters. I prefer burger buns to man buns." Bones shot a baleful gaze at a pair of men wearing skinny jeans, Buddy Holly glasses, and crisp new t-shirts emblazoned with the names of 1980's bands and tour dates. One kept twisting his heavily waxed mustache while the other absently stroked a long but humorously thin beard. "I'll bet you that douche couldn't name three Van Halen songs."

"Never mind," Maddock said. "Let's eat."

The three of them found a booth, each silently processing their own level of discouragement with the lack of progress.

The place was bustling with activity. The waitress, a thirty-something brunette with teased jet-black hair, an ample bosom and full red lips, was late getting to the table, but as busy as it was, the tardiness was forgivable.

"My name is Marlene," she said, smacking her gum. "You know what you want yet?"

Michelle ordered the Portobello Caprese sandwich, and Maddock had the pan-fried trout special. Bones opted for the Full Phoenicia Breakfast: eggs, sausage, bacon, baked beans, tomatoes, potatoes, and toast.

Marlene brought three glasses of ice water, flashed Maddock a smile and whisked herself away.

"So, is this little party over?" Bones asked, addressing the elephant in the room.

"Hell, no! Michelle replied. "It's not over. We push on."

"We've checked out every conceivable lead from the book," Bones protested. "What is left?"

"I didn't think you two were the types to give up," Michelle said.

Maddock had been quiet, reflecting. "Michelle, it's possible that all of this is a legend. All of it. Maybe the reason nobody has found anything is that there's nothing *to* find."

"And it's also possible that someone found that safe years ago and never told anybody," Bones added.

"You don't believe that," she said.

"I don't know what to believe," Maddock replied. "I have to agree with Bones. We've been here for a week now and have followed every possible lead that makes sense. We're getting nowhere."

"What about the leads that don't seem to make sense?" Michelle asked. "Maybe we can spend some time trying to make sense of them."

"Sure. Let's look at one." Bones grabbed Maddock's phone off the table and began scrolling through Jimmy's notes on the last words of Dutch Schultz. "Okay, here you go: *You can play jacks and girls do that with a softball.* Now how would you suggest we go about following that lead?"

"I don't know," she said. "I just think we need to give it more time."

"Dutch was delirious. He was talking out of his ass. It was gibberish—let's face it. I say it's time to move on."

Michelle looked at Maddock, pleading with her eyes.

Maddock shook his head. "I would stay if I thought there was anything productive we could find; any plausible lead we haven't followed. I'm with Bones on this. It's time to call it."

Michelle's face twitched with a combination of frustration, disappointment and anger. Tears glistened in her eyes. She opened her mouth to speak and then closed it again and stood up.

"I'm going to the restroom. Please excuse me."

"I do feel bad for her," Maddock said, when she was well out of earshot.

"You should feel bad for us," Bones replied. "This was a fool's errand—a wild goose chase. I was having a perfectly good time in Atlantic City."

"You were losing your ass in Atlantic City, as I recall. This trip probably saved you from losing another $5,000."

"I was poised for a comeback," he insisted.

"What about the two of you?" Maddock asked. "It looked like there might be something going on."

Bones pursed his lips and waved him off. "You know me. Always touch and go. A little touching, and then it's time to go." He forced a smile.

Maddock chuckled. "One of these days, someone's going to get their hooks in you." Privately, he wasn't certain that would ever happen, but he kept hoping, for his friend's sake.

"It's not going to happen," Bones said. "Definitely not with Michelle."

Maddock stood. "I need to hit the head. I'll be back in a minute."

He headed toward the men's room, which was down a long, under-lit hallway. He was perhaps six feet from the door when something on the wall caught his eye. He stopped looked. There was a framed map encased in glass. It was large, perhaps four feet tall by five feet wide. It looked very old. He began to inspect it. He stood there for more than two minutes, in silence, studying it. Finally, he spoke out loud.

"I'll be damned," he said to himself.

TWELVE

Maddock looked around the restaurant until he spotted the waitress. "Excuse me, Marlene."

"What'cha need, sugar?" she replied with a wide grin. "My telephone number?"

"That's a tempting offer, but I'm actually looking for a little information. Do you know anything about this map?"

She looked at the map. "Nope, not really."

"Is the manager here?" he asked.

"The owner is," she replied. "His name is Mark. Would you like to talk to him?"

Maddock nodded. "I would."

Marlene smiled and walked away. Maddock caught Michelle's attention as she came out of the restroom. He waved her over. She approached as the owner, a non-descript gentleman of fifty or so, arrived,

"Hello, I'm Mark," he said. "Marlene said you were looking to speak to me?" The ghost of a frown on his face suggested he was expecting a customer complaint.

"Yes, I am," Maddock replied. "This map. It looks very old. Can you tell me—is it pre-World War II?"

"It is."

"Where did you get it, if you don't mind my asking?"

"It came from the office of the city planning council here in Phoenicia a long time ago. I like it. Adds to the classic diner ambiance."

Maddock scratched his chin. "About how long ago?"

Mark let out a breath as he thought about it. "Sometime around the year 1940, give or take. The previous owners had this map up in the restaurant long before I bought the place. A lot has changed since then."

"Interesting." Maddock began snapping pictures of the map with his phone, section by section.

"Do you happen to have a yardstick?" he asked.

"Sure, in the back," Mark replied, scratching the top of his balding head. "I'll get it."

"Oh, and could I borrow a dry erase marker too, please?" he added. "The blue one, maybe. The one you use to write out the lunch specials on the white board should work nicely."

As the man walked away, Bones wandered over.

"You two having a party and I wasn't invited?" he asked.

"I have no idea," Michelle asked. "Dane, what is going on with you?"

"When I first saw this old map it hit me," Maddock replied. "We've been processing Dutch's notes from *our modern-day perspective*, over eighty years after he died."

"Okay, so what's your new perspective."

"Dutch made a point for us to *see what the Devil sees*. He also pointed out the Devil faced southeast. So, when we stood on top of the Devil's Face formation and looked southeast, what did we see?"

"Trees," Michelle said.

Bones nodded. "Trees—that's right. Lots and lots of trees and shrubs and bushes."

"But is that what Dutch saw?" Maddock asked. "We see trees *now*, but were those trees there in 1935? And even if they were there, were they as full and as tall as they are today?"

Michelle and Bones looked at each other and shrugged.

"Probably not," Maddock said. "A tree can grow a lot

in eighty years, right? So, if Dutch had climbed to the top of the Devil's Face formation and looked in the direction the Devil faced back in 1935, he may have seen an entirely different view from what we see today."

"The town of Phoenicia has not changed locations," Michelle said. "It was southeast of the Devil's Face formation in 1935 and it still is today."

The owner arrived with a yardstick and a dry erase marker.

"Need anything else?" he asked. "I need to get back to work."

"Thank you, Mark, this is great," Maddock replied. The man smiled and left. Maddock turned back to Michelle.

"You're right, of course," he said. "Phoenicia *is* still in the same place. Tell me, what's the elevation of the Devil's Face formation from the freeway, I mean...approximately?"

Michelle shrugged.

"Bones?"

"Not sure. Maybe three hundred meters," he said.

"That's about what I was thinking, too," Maddock replied. "So, if Dutch was standing high on that hill, on top of the Devil's Face formation, and if the trees were not there or at the very least much shorter, maybe he could see *well beyond Phoenicia*...It's possible even, that the trees were shorter and blocked Phoenicia but did not block what was beyond the town, where the elevation was higher."

"*The devil is a trickster,*" she quoted from Dutch's notes.

"Hand me the book," Maddock said to Michelle. She reached in her bag and pulled the book from it, handing it to him. He flipped through it until he found the page he wanted.

"One of the notes Dutch wrote to Michelle's great-grandmother was this." He read, "*When I see you at Christmas we'll take in the countryside. The train ride has beautiful scenery. I love red.*"

"We checked into this already," Michelle said. "There is no train station in Phoenicia."

"You're right," he said. "There is not a train station in Phoenicia...*today.*"

He opened the dry erase marker and made a blue dot at the location of the Devil's Face formation.

"Are you going to write on this dude's map?" Bones asked.

"Relax. It's covered in glass," Maddock said, "and this is a dry erase marker. That means it erases."

"Just messing with you."

"What if someone is watching?" Michelle said.

"We're down a restroom hallway," Maddock said. "Out of the main line of sight of the dining room."

"You can never be too careful," Bones said.

"We'll erase it, after, I promise," Maddock insisted. "You could always stand at the end of the hall and look scary."

Bones shrugged and kept his eyes on the map.

Maddock created a blue dot at the center of Phoenicia. He placed the yardstick on the glass and drew a straight line from the rock formation to the town. He did not remove the yardstick.

"This is the straight line from the Devil's Face to Phoenicia. The line is going southeast."

Michelle looked at the map. "Okay, your point is?"

"If I draw the line out further, well past Phoenicia, to

the southeast along the exact same path, then it leads to…"

His voice trailed off as he continued to draw the line. It intersected with…

"*The Phoenicia Train Station*," Michelle said, finishing the sentence.

"When Dutch was here in 1935, there *was* a train station, not directly in the town of Phoenicia, but just a few miles southeast, across the Esopus Creek," Maddock said.

Bones studied the map. "So, when Dutch looked out from atop the Devil's Face formation he was looking *past* the town ..."

"And at the train station across the river," Michelle finished. "It's been right in front of us this whole time."

"Maybe...just maybe," Maddock acknowledged.

"There's one thing I still don't understand," Michelle said. "By all accounts Dutch and Lulu *drove their car* that day. They did not take the train. Why would they go to a train station?"

"*The devil is a trickster*," Maddock quoted from the book. "Think about it this way. Let's say you're Dutch and you want to hide the money in a place that no one would ever find. You might be worried about someone retracing your steps for that day. Maybe he thought he was being followed. It's possible that he made trips to Phoenicia, Esopus Creek and to Devil's Face for the sole purpose of misdirection."

"Maybe he was looking for a great place to hide the loot and decides against all three places, but when he reaches Devil's Face ..." Bones trailed off.

"He sees the train station," Michelle said, completing Bones' sentence.

"Or just the opposite," Maddock said. "Suppose he intended to hide the safe at the train station all along. He looks up and sees the Devil's Face formation from the train station. He sees the formation facing him, watching him."

"Wow," Bones said. "That's different."

"I agree," Maddock said. "And knowing that people might try to retrace his steps, he realizes that people will know he traveled by *car* ... "

"Making the train station a perfect spot for hiding money," Michelle finished. "No one would think to look there. He *was driving a car*, after all. Why would anyone suspect he would hide money in a train station? And it's a great landmark for when they decide to come back for it, later."

"But horrible for us when it closed decades ago," Maddock added.

"What does *I love red* mean?" Michelle asked.

Maddock shrugged. "No idea. Maybe the safe is red. Maybe the door to the room where the safe is stored is red...We'll have to figure that out. The more pressing question is, what remains of that old station today? Was it leveled? Is it a parking lot?"

Maddock walked down the hall and scanned the restaurant for the owner. He saw Mark and made eye contact. Mark finished a coffee refill for a customer and approached.

"Excuse me, Mark," Maddock asked. "Do you have any idea if the old train station building is still there?"

"It's considered a historic landmark. It's been preserved. That's where the Empire State Railway Museum is."

"So, it's a museum now?" Maddock asked for

clarification.

"Yep, it's a nice place to take the kids," he said, walking away.

"Son of a gun," Michelle said, beaming at Maddock. "You did it."

"Maybe," Maddock said, shrugging it off. "We haven't found anything yet."

"But this is by far our most promising lead," Bones said.

"If it's a historic landmark, that means the curators would do everything they could to maintain its original look and feel," Michelle said. "It's possible the safe's final resting place has never been disturbed."

He looked at Bones. "So what do you think partner? You still want to give up and go home?"

Bones grinned. "Screw that. I'm all in. Let's erase this blue line and get the hell out of here."

THIRTEEN

As they finished their meal, Michelle looked up information on the Phoenicia Railroad on her smartphone. "Our new theory is holding up," she said.

"Excuse me, *our* new theory?" Maddock scoffed.

"You know what I mean," she replied. "The railroad was in full service in 1935. Passenger service was not discontinued until 1954. For thirty-one years the station had sat, totally abandoned. The building was left to deteriorate until a Railroad enthusiast bought the property and turned it into a museum, which opened in 1985. It became listed on the National Register of Historic Places and had been restored to its original look and feel."

"You find anything else of interest?" Maddock asked.

"We'll take a look at Dutch's notes again with a fresh set of eyes tonight," Michellez said. "Now that we have a better idea of what we are looking for, maybe some of the notes will make more sense."

"The book has clearly made the difference," Bones said to Michelle. "None of the public information referred to seeing what the Devil saw or to trains."

"You're right," Maddock said. "Without that book, we'd be as blind as everyone else was."

"Let's get back to the hotel," Michelle said. "I'll spring for a six-pack of cold brew. We'll take it out on the patio of my room and go through the notes in the book one more time."

"Sounds good," Maddock said. "We'll get a fresh start in the morning."

Birdwatcher's eyes closely followed the trio as they walked out to their car and drove away. For the first time since beginning his covert surveillance, he did not bother to follow them. Instead, he rose from his table in the corner of the diner and walked over to the restroom area, heading down the long hallway. It didn't take him long to find what they had been looking at.

He studied the map carefully. There was a chalk tray underneath it and a blue dry erase marker lying on it. Beside it was a yardstick. He sighed and shook his head. It was not immediately obvious what spot on the map had drawn their interest, but it was easy enough to figure out what they had been trying to do.

He pulled a pocket flashlight from his pocket and shone it on the glass. The light revealed the still-moist residue of ink recently wiped clean. A smeared line appeared to begin at the Devil's Face formation and ended at the Phoenicia Train Station.

Birdwatcher knew there was no longer a train station in Phoenicia.

Why would they be interested in an abandoned train station? he wondered. He remembered seeing Maddock speaking to the manager.

Birdwatcher went back to his table and called for his waitress. She smiled as she approached.

"Could I have my check please?" he asked.

"No dessert?" she replied.

"Not tonight, thank you," he replied. "However, could you ask the manager to stop by my table? I'd love to pass my regards to him for the good food and lovely service."

Her eyes widened. "You bet. I'll get him."

Two minutes later the manager approached him,

smiling. He introduced himself. Birdwatcher spent a moment praising the excellent cuisine and extraordinary service, though in truth he had found the service barely tolerable and the food barely edible. The manager beamed.

"You know, I will be in Phoenicia for another day," Birdwatcher went on. "I am a bit of a railroad enthusiast. I know there was a railroad station here at one time. Whatever became of it?"

Mark smiled. "Wow! You're the second person tonight who has asked about that. It's now a museum."

Birdwatcher raised his eyebrows. "A museum? Really?"

"Yep, it's called the Empire State Railway Museum."

"How interesting," he said. "Thank you."

The manager smiled and walked away. Birdwatcher waited until he was gone then picked up his cell and dialed. The phone was answered on the first ring.

"You have news?" Virtuoso asked.

"I do," he said. "I think they may be close to finding the safe at the Empire State Railway Museum."

"A train museum?" Virtuoso repeated. "That doesn't seem likely."

"I saw their reactions," Birdwatcher replied. "They came into the restaurant dejected. They discovered an old map on the wall. They left elated. I'm convinced they are on to something."

"Good," came the reply. "You think they will find the safe soon, then?"

"Very soon would be my guess," Birdwatcher replied.

"Do they have any idea you have eyes on them?" he asked.

"None at all."

"Are you certain?" Virtuoso pressed.

"I'm certain," he replied. "I've been sitting in a booth twenty feet away from them, and they've not so much as given a glance in this direction."

"Good. I will send my team in tomorrow," Virtuoso said. "Once they find the safe, my men will move in and claim it. You are then free to eliminate our three problems."

"You're sending your men in tomorrow—*before* we know for sure they have found the safe?"

"Yes, I want them on hand as the safe is being discovered. They will swoop in and take control."

"I'm okay with that as long as they do not try to kill Maddock," Birdwatcher said firmly.

"That sounds suspiciously like you are giving *me* an order," Virtuoso said. "Maybe we should refresh ourselves on this particular employer-employee relationship we have going here. I'm calling the shots, or did you forget that?"

"Call it a reminder regarding your contractual obligation," Birdwatcher countered.

"I'm not sure I like your tone," Virtuoso said stiffly.

"My tone is not relevant. I expect you to honor your commitment."

"You worry about doing your job, how's that?" Virtuoso said. "Just make sure none of them leave there alive."

"I know my job and I do it well. That's why you hired me," he assured and then hung up.

Pompous American ass, he thought.

He glanced in the direction that the trio had headed, thinking about Maddock. He decided on the spot that a long-range shot to the head would *never do*. He wanted Maddock to *see him*, to look into his eyes, to *know* who had killed him. That would mean using a pistol, rather than a rifle. He would have to get close. It would increase the chances of him being caught.

He smiled. It was worth the risk.

FOURTEEN

Maddock, Bones, and Michelle were fifteen minutes away from the Empire State Railway Museum, the former Phoenicia Train Station. Michelle drove and Bones sat in the passenger's seat. Maddock was sitting in the back, considering options, when his phone rang—it was Jimmy Letson.

"I have some news you will want to hear," Letson began. His voice sounded anxious.

"Go ahead," replied Maddock.

"I know who the other interested parties are," he said. "The ones who posed as FBI agents and killed Michelle's mother in search of the book, the same ones who sent the man posing as a taxi driver to kill you."

"Tell me," Maddock said, perking up.

"Before he died, Dutch Schultz handed the copy of *Mary Poppins* to a man named Alex Singer, correct?" Letson asked.

"Yes, Singer was the brother of Michelle's great-grandmother," Maddock replied. "The theory is that Dutch knew he was going to die and didn't want to put Michelle's great-grandmother in danger, so he gave the book to her brother for delivery."

"Well, in addition to him being the brother of Michelle's great-grandmother, Alex Singer was a war hero in WWI," Letson said. "He was awarded the Distinguished Service Cross and the Silver Star for his brave service during the Second Battle of the Marne in 1918. He died in 1955."

"Look, Jimmy, I know this is all leading to a point," Maddock said, "but I'm not making the connection."

"Hey, do you want to hear the story or not?" Letson said. "Don't get your shorts in a bunch. I'm getting there. Alex had a son, Steven Singer, born in 1940. Steven was a military man himself and very proud of his father's service record. He wrote his dad's biography, called *Singer of the Marne*. It was published two years ago For what it's worth, it didn't sell well. But it sold well enough to draw one man's attention."

"Okay," Maddock said, still not understanding the relevance.

"In this book, Steven described all of his father's military exploits and heroics, but *also* offered his father's *personal insights*. Some of those insights reflected experiences he had *after the war*."

Maddock was beginning to get the picture. "Now I'm interested. Tell me more."

"*Now* you're interested. Screw you, Maddock. Anyway, in one of the chapters of the book Steven retells a story his father had told him many times: the story of how he had met the notorious Dutch Schultz just hours before his death, and that Dutch had given him money for his sister, who was pregnant at the time. He also writes that Dutch gave him a *book* to be given to Alex's sister as a birthday present."

"The first edition of *Mary Poppins*?" Maddock asked. "He mentioned the book by name in the biography?"

"He did, and also that the book contained, and I now quote, '*all manner of personal, handwritten notes from the Dutchman.*' He goes on to say, '*while personal in nature, the notes seemed nonsensical, almost as if written in code.*'"

"In code? Holy crap," Maddock exclaimed. "Anyone interested in Dutch's treasure would not have to go far to make that connection. Did the book mention the name or home town of Michelle's great-grandmother?"

"Nope. I'm getting to that. There's more," Letson said. "Six months ago, Steven Singer was murdered. It was well planned. Steven had no enemies; the authorities could find no one with any motivation to kill him."

"You think the murder was related?" Maddock asked.

"Hell yes," Letson replied. "A week prior to his death, Steve Singer reported that men showed up at his house claiming to be FBI agents, asking for more details about the book and about Alex's sister. They were especially interested in her name and where she lived. Steven grew suspicious and called the FBI."

"Let me guess," Maddock interrupted. "The men questioning Steven were not FBI."

"You got it," Letson replied. "A week later, Steven Singer was found dead. His body showed evidence of torture."

"Did the FBI come up with any suspects?" Maddock asked.

"Yes, the FBI found the bullet used to kill Steven. They traced its manufacturing back to Europe—specifically France."

"France?"

"Yes, France."

Maddock groaned. This news was bound to elicit plenty of anti-French wisecracks from Bones.

"The FBI suspects the hit was made by a paid assassin—the job was too professional to be otherwise."

"It's the Birdwatcher—dammit. I know him," Maddock replied. "I crossed paths with him when I served in the Navy. He's a cold-blooded murderer. I have a personal history with him—it's not pleasant."

"Birdwatcher was the name I came up with as well," Letson said. "I just don't know why they'd bother to kill Steven if they had the information they came for."

"Because they didn't want him passing the name and hometown of Michelle's grandmother on to the real FBI or to other treasure seekers," Maddock said.

"So, now we know how these people found the whereabouts of the book," Letson said.

"Birdwatcher doesn't work for free and has no interest in buried treasure," Maddock said. "Someone is financing this."

"You're right. I did some more poking around and got a hit. Birdwatcher works for a man known as Virtuoso," Letson said.

That name rang a bell for Maddock, too. He knew the man was a mob boss but remembered little else. He asked Letson for background.

"Virtuoso is the nickname for Anthony Rossi," Letson said. "The nickname comes from the efficient, creative and artistic manner in which he eliminates his enemies. Rossi is the boss of one of New York's largest Mafia rings, and a grand-nephew of Lucky Luciano, the very same mob boss who ordered the hit on Dutch Schultz."

"That can't be a coincidence," Maddock noted.

"You're right," Letson said. "Rossi has long been obsessed with Dutch Schultz folklore and the whereabouts of his lost treasure. He has hired and financed treasure hunting crews on three separate occasions to find Dutch's safe—with no luck, obviously."

"Isn't Virtuoso on the FBI's Most Wanted list?" Maddock asked.

"Yep," Letson replied. "Top five. Virtuoso has never been caught and continues to run his organization from remote locations. He frequently moves from place to place. The Feds have not gotten a bead on his hideout in over two years. You are now on both his and Birdwatcher's radar. I'd be very careful."

"Always. You say Steven Singer was killed six months ago?" Maddock asked.

"Yes," Letson replied.

"Thanks, Jimmy," Maddock said. "Good work. You're a life-saver—literally."

Maddock hung up and brought Michelle and Bones up to speed, sharing every detail of his conversation with Jimmy Letson.

"It all fits Michelle's timeline," Maddock explained. "Men posing as FBI agents showed up at her mother's door four months ago looking for the book. They killed her and ransacked the house looking for it. They then ransacked Michelle's house as well. One of Rossi's goons tried to kill us in Atlantic City."

"Was the cab driver the Birdwatcher?" Michelle asked.

"No, it wasn't. The cab driver was someone else," Maddock replied. "My first guess is that the Virtuoso thought it was going to be an easy job finding and handling a single unarmed woman and didn't feel the need to send out the big guns. He opted to send a lower level guy to do the job but we showed up and spoiled the party."

"That's probably right," Bones said.

"That sexist jerk!" Michelle snarled.

"You're upset that Rossi didn't send his best guy to kill us?" Bones asked.

"No...that's not what I meant," she said.

"What else could you have meant?" Bones snapped.

"Rossi will not make the same mistake twice," Maddock added, moving the conversation along.

"Do you think ...?" Michelle began.

Maddock nodded, anticipating her question. "I'd be willing to bet the Birdwatcher has been following our every move since we got here."

"You took precautions to make sure we weren't followed," Michelle said.

"Birdwatcher can find us if he wants to."

"How do you know so much about this Birdwatcher anyway?" Michelle asked Maddock. "How do you know him?"

"Our paths crossed when I was in the military," Maddock said. "I saw his handiwork a few times when I served in the Navy as a SEAL. Our interactions were...confrontational. Let's just say after we met I never got a Christmas card from him."

"Why didn't he just kill us and take the book?" Bones asked.

"Simple. He needs us to find the safe for him," Maddock replied. "Virtuoso must have tried to find the safe several times and failed. Letson said Alex Singer's son was tortured for information before he was killed. That has to be how they found out about Michelle's mother and where she lived. Virtuoso suspects that the book contains clues to the location of Dutch's treasure. My bet is he's keeping tabs on us until *we* locate the safe. When we find it, his plan will be to swoop in, kill us and take the safe and its contents."

"So, how do we look for the safe and avoid being killed?" Bones asked.

"Maybe we divert our route right now," Michelle suggested. "There's a lot of traffic on this road now, but you have to believe he's following us. What if we provide a little misdirection and go someplace different until we can find a way to get him off our tail?"

Maddock thought for a moment. "That might work except for one small problem," he said. "In my sheer enthusiasm last night, I drew a line on a map in a public restaurant right to where we are heading. I'll lay odds that the Birdwatcher had eyes on us from somewhere."

"I did warn you," Bones said.

"You erased the line on the map," Michelle said. "We were in a hallway. He couldn't have seen it."

"Yeah, but we talked to the manager about the museum," Maddock said.

"Dammit!" Bones exclaimed. "You're right. He already knows where we're going to be. He's too smart not to."

"What do we do?" Michelle asked.

"We find the treasure as planned," Maddock said.

"What about the Birdwatcher?"

"We have one advantage," Maddock said. "He doesn't know we know he's following us."

"How is that an advantage?" Michelle asked.

"I don't know," Maddock said. "I'm making this up as I go."

FIFTEEN

The Empire State Railway Museum was a simple, shotgun house-style building with an oversized roof. Its awning cast shadows over the wooden platform that ran along the front. The rectangular shaped stone structure was sided in wood shingles with the window frames and awnings painted a mint green color. Its peaked roof was shingled in asphalt, with a large chimney on the west side. The gold plaque in the front indicated the building was constructed in 1899. Above the ticket windows hung a hand-lettered sign that read PHOENICIA. All around were old train relics—engines, passenger cars freight cars, with tourists milling all around.

Michelle and Bones kept scoping out the cars arriving behind them, hoping to identify the Birdwatcher.

"You see him?" Michelle asked Bones.

"I don't see a thing," Bones said, turning to Maddock. "You?"

Maddock shook his head.

"We don't know for sure he is following us, do we?" Michelle asked.

"Oh, he's here somewhere, I'd bet money on it," Maddock responded. "He's a long-range sniper by trade. I'll wager he has eyes on us this very moment using high-powered binoculars."

"Or in his rifle sights," Bones added.

Michelle instinctively began looking around.

"Don't bother," Maddock said. "He's a pro. If he doesn't want to be seen, you won't see him. If you look too much he will know we are aware of his presence."

"This is making me really nervous, guys," Michelle said.

"As well it should," Maddock said. "The man is a murderer, a cold-blooded assassin. He won't try to hurt us until he knows we have found the safe. He also doesn't know that we know he is here."

"Do we know what he looks like, this Birdwatcher?" Michelle asked.

"It's been a long time since I've seen him," Maddock said. "I'm not sure I'd recognize his face now. But he gets his nickname from the clothes he wears. He carries these giant high-powered binoculars, so he dresses as a birdwatcher to avoid suspicion from people seeing him walking around with them draped around his neck."

"So, the high-powered sniper rifle he carries doesn't give anyone a clue?" Bones asked.

"The rifle comes later, after he's scoped out his target," Maddock replied. "He typically gets close to his targets and learns about them—he does his diligence."

"So, look for safari-type clothing?" Michelle asked.

"Oh, and one more thing. The man has an affinity for Payday candy bars."

"What?" she asked. "That was totally random."

"Back when I knew the guy, he always carried a pocket filled with Payday candy bars."

"That's helpful. Now we know he doesn't have a peanut allergy," Bones said with a smirk.

Maddock ignored him. "We'll split off in two directions. He can't follow us both."

"What if he's not alone?" Bones said.

"He will be. Birdwatcher always works by himself. He trusts no one."

"Who will he follow?" Michelle asked.

"He hates me with a passion and wants me dead," Maddock replied.

"Why does he hate you so much?" Michelle asked.

"The last time I saw him, I smacked him down and humiliated him in front of a group of his buddies," Maddock said. "He threatened to kill me then and there but it would have been hard to do with us being on a joint mission at the time. Technically, we were on the same side. I saw the hate in his eyes, though. I'm sure I'll be his first target."

"We can't let you go alone," Michelle said.

"Oh, I won't be alone," Maddock replied. He pulled his pistol from his belt line at the small of his back. "This little guy will keep me company."

"You have a gun?" Michelle exclaimed.

"Comes in handy at times," Maddock replied.

"No offense, but that Walther is pretty short range," Bones said. "Birdwatcher has a high-powered rifle."

"There are over a hundred people in this place," Maddock replied. "Remember, he doesn't know we know he's tailing us. He's going to keep tabs on us from the perimeter. He needs to make sure we've found the safe before he makes a move. It's going to be my job to identify his position while we are looking for the safe."

"And how do you plan to pull that off?" Bones asked.

Maddock shrugged. "I have an idea. I'm still working on it, but it will be an actual plan pretty soon."

"What happens if we actually find the safe?" Michelle asked. "Or if he just thinks we've found it?"

"First, he'll probably let Virtuoso know. Then he'll, find a position on high ground, wait for us to show our faces, then put a bullet in each one of our heads," Bones replied.

"You think he'll just shoot us first chance he gets?" Michelle asked. "Without waiting for us to find the safe?"

"No," Bones said. "As long as he doesn't suspect we know he's there, I think he'll opt to take us out in the car once we've left here. That's what I'd do if I were him. We would be all in one confined place and away from the crowd. If he shoots us here at the museum there will be lots of panic. People screaming, general pandemonium. The police will swarm the place. There would be no way Virtuoso's men could extract the safe with the authorities here."

"I think Bones is right," Maddock said.

She nodded. "Okay, then. Where do we start?"

"We get the lay of the land," Maddock said. "Bones, you take the museum building. That's the renovated train station itself, and it has two dozen people moving about it, inside and out. Michelle, you go with Bones. You're safest inside the building. Stay clear of the windows. I'll draw Birdwatcher away from the crowds by searching the property."

"That's dangerous," Bones said. "Birdwatcher is not a man to be messed with. Maybe I should go with you."

"No, Bones. In case I'm wrong and he kills me and heads your direction, I need you to protect Michelle."

Bones pulled his Glock from his belt line at the small of his back.

"You have a gun, too?" Michelle blurted. "Everyone has a gun but me. Why is that?"

"Have you ever shot a pistol before?" Bones asked.

"No."

"So, there's your first clue."

She frowned at Bones, then turned back toward Maddock.

"I hope you know what you're doing."

"That makes two of us," he replied.

"What exactly are we looking for?" Michelle asked.

"If we're lucky, you'll know it when you see it," Maddock said. "Perhaps there is an old storage room. Maybe they had storage lockers. Oh, there is another thing. Try to find out if there is a long-time employee working; someone who has been associated with this place for many years. Ask him about the history of the building—renovations, that kind of thing. Communicate with me by cell phone. Are we ready?"

Bones and Michelle nodded.

"Good. Let's go find some treasure," Maddock said.

"I still don't understand how we live through this if we do find it." Michelle said.

"Leave that to me," he said. "I have a plan. You two go ahead. I need to make a quick call. I'll be right behind you."

Bones then turned to Michelle.

"Have some faith. He might be a short, little pretty boy, but Maddock knows what he's doing." He looked at Maddock with widened eyes as if to say, *You do know what you're doing, right?*

Michelle and Bones slowly approached the front of the museum building. To the left of the front door was a two-passenger handcar.

"I've always wanted to ride one of those," Bones said.

"Not me. Too much work."

Inside, Michelle admired the way the building had been preserved. The waiting area for the passengers was largely intact, as was the ticket office. Yet, she noted, they still managed to find plenty of area to sell souvenirs.

Bones spotted a tour guide. He nudged Michelle and pointed him out. The man had to have been in his seventies, Bones thought—perhaps even eighty. He was dressed as a passenger car ticket-taker. He wore a double-breasted dark suit that displayed a gold chain leading to his pocket where it was undoubtedly attached to a gold pocket watch. His ensemble was completed by a flat-topped navy-blue railroad hat. He looked at them through wire-rimmed glasses with lenses as thick as soda bottles, and flashed a friendly smile as Michelle approached him. She looked at his name badge. It read Raymond Wigg.

"Hi Mr. Wigg, my name is Michelle," she greeted. "This is my friend Uriah."

He smiled at Bones who gave a cursory nod. "And what can I do for you today, Michelle?"

"We are historic building enthusiasts."

"Well, this one's a dandy," he beamed.

"So, you know a lot about this building?"

"I've been here for more than twenty years as an employee," he said. "I was a regular visitor here for twenty years before that. I've been a railroad enthusiast for as long as I can remember. I've seen this place turned into the museum from an abandoned railway junkyard."

"Wow. You've been around this place for forty years?"

He winked at her. "Indeed."

She beamed. "I see I've found the right person. What can you tell me about it?" she asked. "How much of what I see is original?"

"Well, the structure itself was built in 1899. Inside, the station kept most of its original layout. Between the two rooms on the trackside is the ticket agent's office, which retains its brass window bars and milk glass windows. The benches, water fountain and sink that are in the waiting room along with the oversized heating grate—all are original."

"Wow! You *do* know a lot about this building," she replied. She smiled warmly.

"I do," he said, returning the smile.

"Tell me, Raymond," Bones interjected. "Isn't it common for train stations to have public storage lockers? I don't see any here."

"Modern-day train stations certainly do, but this one was built before the turn of the 19th century before the powers that be thought of such things, so no—no lockers."

"Do you think you could give me a backroom tour, you know, to the areas not generally seen by the public?" Michelle asked. She touched his arm lightly.

"Oh certainly," he said, his cheeks turning a slight shade of red. "Right this way."

Raymond took Michelle and Bones through all the back areas, explaining that the build-out of the new electrical room was one of the very few changes that had been made. Michelle smiled and asked questions, which Raymond seemed more than happy to answer.

"You know, Mr. Wigg ..."

"Please...call me Raymond," he interrupted.

"Raymond... my friend and I are also interested in turn-of-the-century relics, like old printing presses, typesetting machines, old office equipment—perhaps even old...safes. Do you have anything like that around?"

"Hmmm," he emoted, scratching his chin. "There's nothing like that I can think of."

"Perhaps in an old storage area?" she asked.

He thought for another moment. "Nope. If there were things like that here, I'd know about them."

Her smile was cordial but empty.

SIXTEEN

Maddock circled around the rear of the station to the building's west side. He pulled his cell from his pocket and made a call. Jimmy Letson answered on the second ring.

"I need you to listen to me carefully," Maddock said. "I have some instructions that require precise timing."

"Sure," he replied. Maddock was relieved that Jimmy had read his tone of voice and not responded with one of his trademark jibes. "Tell me what you want."

"I need you to make a call on my behalf ..." he began.

He continued to survey the grounds as he began telling Jimmy what he wanted him to do.

Nearby stood a mini train station, designed for children's rides. A couple of large family groups were waiting for the train to arrive. Maddock decided to move away from the area as quickly as possible. If Birdwatcher was following him, he wanted to identify his position and confront him. He wanted as few people around as possible, particularly children.

He turned his attention back to his phone conversation. He could tell by the pauses that Jimmy was taking notes as they spoke.

He looked off at the tree groves surrounding the station. The good news was, if he was able to find Birdwatcher and confront him, it would likely be far away from the crowds. The bad news was, the assassin could be watching him from almost anywhere.

The children's station looked new, as though it had been constructed in the last few years. There was a remote possibility that Dutch Schultz had buried the safe in the dirt and simply used the station as a landmark for finding it again later. If so, it was quite possible that a new structure had been built over it, making recovery impossible, but Maddock didn't think that was the case.

It was unlikely Dutch would have taken the time to bury the safe. Most of the ground in and around Phoenicia was hard and rocky. Digging a hole wide and deep enough to cover a safe would have been laborious, especially for two men who were said to have been wearing suits that day. They would have also been wearing heavy coats since it was October when the average temperature was barely above freezing. Digging a hole in the rocky ground while wearing a business suit and a heavy overcoat would have been dirty sweaty work. Moreover, Dutch knew his time was short. The FBI was closing in. The mob wanted him dead. If he were able to escape danger, he would have wanted to access the money quickly and easily. All of this pointed to the possibility that the safe was not buried in the ground.

Maddock moved to the north side of the building as he finished the conversation with Jimmy. He looked at his watch; it was eleven-eighteen.

"Okay, I've got it. You sure that's what you want done?" Jimmy asked.

"I'm sure," Maddock replied. "Remember, timing is critical."

"I'm on it," he said.

"Thanks Jimmy," he said. "You've been incredible."

Maddock hit the end button on his cell. He turned his attention once again to the potential whereabouts of the safe. On the north side of the building he saw several interesting possibilities.

There were several flat railroad cars that looked older, but most likely still built well after Dutch's death in 1935. He could rule those out. There was an ancient-looking rusted side dump car, used to carry coal. He would want to check out that car and its surroundings. He saw a yellow and green transfer caboose, again, probably built in the World War II era, 1945-ish or a little later. He could rule that out as well.

He wondered if the museum had logs indicating when the railroad cars arrived at the museum. If he could find such a record, he could eliminate everything that was built after 1935, or that arrived after the year Dutch was killed. He made a mental note to seek out an administrative office or storage room where they kept old records.

He also noted a corroded braced boxcar, used for transporting livestock. Maddock had no idea how long ago it had been built or had been resting there, but the grass and weeds growing around was telling—it had been there for a very long time.

He noticed a passenger car that had been covered with cloth. He would certainly want to inspect that car as well as an ancient-looking gold commuter car.

I love red, he thought. That's what Dutch wrote.

None of the dilapidated cars were red or even had red trim or doors. He saw lots of brown cars and wondered if any of them had once been red but long since faded. He did see two passenger cars that were red, but in both cases, he was fairly certain they had been built years after Dutch was alleged to have hidden the treasure—no help.

He looked at his watch again: eight minutes had passed.

He was just about to call Bones for a status update when he saw a blinding reflection from off in the distance.

The searing reflection appeared to be coming from the trees more than a hundred yards away.

A reflection from *polished glass*, perhaps?

Perhaps a glass *lens*.

A lens from a pair of *binoculars*, maybe? Or a rifle sight.

The *Birdwatcher*. Maddock had found him.

SEVENTEEN

The Birdwatcher smiled as he saw Maddock looking in his direction. It was a sunny day. He knew there was a risk that the reflection from his binoculars would give his position away, and it had. He was all right with it. Maddock knew he was being watched and now knew *where* he was being watched *from*. He wasn't certain yet that Maddock knew *who* was doing the watching, but he intended to proceed as though his identity had been exposed as well.

It didn't look like Maddock or the others had found the Dutchman's safe, but he was not about to wait any longer. Now that he had been spotted, he needed to strike. He knew Maddock would come for him...

Away from the crowds ...

Away from his friends ...

Exactly what he wanted.

First, he would look Maddock in the eye, and watch for his reaction as he realized he was about to die. He would then kill him. Time permitting, he would gag him and shoot him in the liver, allowing his death to be slow and excruciatingly painful. If he lived for too long afterward, he'd finish Maddock with a bullet through his ear...or better yet, through his eye. Afterward, he would kill Maddock's two friends. He would make up a story for Virtuoso that somehow explained why he had to kill them before they actually found the safe.

And if Virtuoso didn't believe him and made a fuss, Birdwatcher would kill him too, and then slip off into the night with the book in hand. Maybe he'd even consider hiring treasure hunters of his own, but those were thoughts for another time.

Right now, he intended to confront Maddock face to face and kill him. He had made a good decision, he thought. He was more certain than ever that a head shot from his rifle at one hundred yards would never do—it would not be a death satisfying enough to avenge the embarrassment Maddock had caused him.

One hundred yards away, Maddock hid from Birdwatcher's view behind an old railroad car, pulled the pistol from his belt at his lower back waistline. He called Bones from his cell. "Are you inside the building?"

"Yeah, but we're striking out," Bones said.

"Stay inside and away from the windows. I've spotted Birdwatcher's position. He is up a hill about a hundred yards northeast of the building. Do not come out. Take care of Michelle."

"Don't go it alone," Bones insisted. "It's too dangerous. I know you can handle yourself but this guy kills for a living. He doesn't think twice. On top of that, you're probably outgunned."

"I have to end this, now," Maddock said. "I have to do it myself. I'm going to close the gap. I'd rather face him at close range than be a moving target from a distance."

"Let me come with you," Bones said.

"No, you have to protect Michelle," he said. "If he does get past me, then you are all that stands between him and Michelle."

"You'll be a sitting duck," Bones said.

"Hopefully, a moving duck," Maddock said.

"You really need to rethink this."

"Trust me. This is hardly the first time one of us has

flown solo. Wish me luck," Maddock said. "Gotta go."

"Good luck, asshat," Bones said.

Maddock hung up. There was a grove within a hundred feet of his position. If he could make it to that tree line, he was confident he could make it the rest of the way to Birdwatcher's position without being seen. He casually strolled toward the nearest tree line, pretending to be interested in the layout of the area. When he reached the grove, he ducked into the thickness of the trees.

He hid behind a large maple, taking a peek to reestablish the last known position of the Birdwatcher. He guessed that the French assassin would remain in place for only a short while if his target didn't reemerge into the open. He estimated that he could make his way to Birdwatcher in five to seven minutes taking the long way around. But would the sniper still be there?

He checked his pistol one last time, and then after one last look took off. He trotted silently at a brisk pace up the hillside, careful to stay hidden.

Once he was on the hill Maddock began heading toward Birdwatcher's last known position. He was hoping to circle that position and approach him from behind. If Birdwatcher did move, Maddock thought, he would likely move in toward the building trying to reacquire his target's positions.

Maddock sensed something moving nearby. He couldn't see anyone, but he knew someone was there. He moved to his left, putting a tree between himself and the spot where he knew someone waited. He listened, and finally heard just the faint scuff of a shoe on soft earth. The person was moving off again. It had to be Birdwatcher.

Maddock moved in the direction he anticipated the man to be headed. He moved silently. Bones would have approved.

And then he heard the sound again, but behind him. He ducked behind cover. Birdwatcher was good. He'd managed to change directions without Maddock seeing him. This was going to be tougher than he'd thought.

The game of cat and mouse went on for several minutes, each aware of the other but unable to gain an advantage. Finally, Maddock arrived very near to the spot where he'd registered the reflection from the binoculars. There was no sign of Birdwatcher anywhere, but he did see a loose paper lying on the ground near the boulder, crumpled in a wad. He walked over and picked it up.

A *Payday candy bar wrapper*—it *was* him. It was the first real verification. Birdwatcher had been here, in this very spot.

The question was, where was he now?

He pulled his cell phone out and checked the time, then punched several buttons on his phone and slipped it back into his pocket.

He saw movement in his peripheral vision and inched forward quietly, heading back in the direction of the train station, keeping an eye on the spot he guessed that the man would be.

He guessed wrong.

"Don't take another step, Maddock." The voice was baritone, laced with a thick French accent. And it was impossibly close.

Maddock spun, grabbed the man's wrist and forced it to the side as Birdwatcher pulled the trigger. The bullet missed. Maddock tried to bring his own weapon to bear but Birdwatcher caught him in a similar grip.

They grappled in a macabre dance of death. Eye to eye, turning slowly. Each looking for a momentary advantage. Maddock attempted a headbutt, but Birdwatcher turned his head and caught only a glancing blow to the jawbone, then replied with a knee that just missed Maddock's groin.

"Look at me," Birdwatcher said in a low growl. "This is the true devil's face. It's the last thing you will see before you die."

Maddock hadn't seen the man in more than a decade. Birdwatcher's skin was leathered with age and red, burned from sun exposure, no doubt the consequence of days spent keeping watch on Maddock and his friends.

"You've definitely gotten uglier," Maddock said. "But the devil? I don't know. More like the south end of a north-facing baboon."

Birdwatcher sneered. "Your insults do nothing to help your position, Maddock."

"Like your position's any better." He attempted an outside leg trip but Birdwatcher managed to remain on his feet and keep his grip on his weapon and on Maddock's wrist. "You've gotten soft."

"Shut up," Birdwatcher said through gritted teeth.

"That's what cheap junk food will do to you."

Birdwatcher threw his weight forward. Maddock's heel caught on a low lying branch and he nearly lost his balance.

"Nice try. You almost got me."

"Just give me the book."

"Seriously?" Maddock grunted beneath the man's weight. "Do you believe I would bring the honey to the bear?"

"Who has it?" he demanded. "The woman?"

Maddock didn't answer. He wanted to keep talking. As long as he didn't make a mistake, he was certain he could outlast Birdwatcher. He just needed time.

"Your friend, perhaps—Bones, is it?"

"So, how much is Virtuoso paying you to kill me and recover the book?" Maddock asked.

Birdwatcher said nothing, but the look on his face told Maddock he had surprised the Frenchman with the knowledge that he knew who had financed this operation.

"Cat got your tongue, bird brain?" Maddock taunted. "Didn't think I knew about Anthony Rossi, did you?"

Birdwatcher remained silent. He wore the strain of their struggle on his face. Lips tight, sweat pouring from his brow. "You know nothing."

"He didn't offer to pay you a percentage of the proceeds from Dutch's treasure, did he?"

Birdwatcher's eyes flared.

Maddock chuckled. "That's it, isn't it? Well, Birdman, congratulations. You just got screwed big time."

"What do you mean?" he said.

"I mean, the train station was our last hope," Maddock replied. "We found nothing. It's not here. We struck out."

"You're lying," Birdwatcher barked. He made a sudden, frantic move to try and pull his gun hand free, but Maddock held on. It wasn't easy. Both men were now slicked with sweat.

"You've been following us all week, bird beak,"

Maddock snapped. "You've seen us looking—dead end after dead end. This was the final stop—last chance Texaco."

"You're going to die," Birdwatcher said.

"Promises, promises." Maddock still couldn't quite believe they were having this conversation while locked in this deadly stalemate.

"I can think of three possibilities," Maddock said. "Someone else found the treasure long ago and chose to keep it secret; or Dutch intentionally put out false clues to send everyone down the wrong path and we'll never find it."

"You said *three* possibilities," Birdwatcher reminded him.

"Or...and this is the one I believe, there was *never* any buried treasure to begin with," Maddock stated, matter-of-factly. "It was all legend."

"I'm going to kill you. Then, I will kill your friends and take the book. After that, we'll see for certain if you're lying."

"We will indeed," a heavy voice with a thick New York-Italian accent called out from behind Birdwatcher.

The French assassin didn't bother to turn around. He knew Virtuoso's voice. Maddock saw the Mafia kingpin moving toward him, flanked by three of his men on the left side and four on the right. Each of the men carried a semi-automatic weapon.

"Both of you drop your weapons. Now!"

Maddock and Birdwatcher complied. As their pistols struck the soft earth, they ceased their grappling match and backed away from one another.

"I didn't expect you to make a personal appearance," Birdwatcher said.

"I'm full of surprises," Rossi replied.

Virtuoso was in his mid-fifties. His face was heavily lined; his glasses had oversized darkened lenses. His hair was short, perfectly coiffed in a slicked back style. His Italian suit cost more than the credit limit on Maddock's Visa card.

He held a Crimson Trace revolver, pointed at Maddock's head.

"You're Maddock, right?" he said, as though he were making a casual observation.

"I am."

"You said you'd leave Maddock to me," Birdwatcher said.

"Yeah, about that," Rossi replied, turning back toward the assassin. "There has been a change of plan. I'm going in a new direction."

"What do you mean?" Birdwatcher demanded.

"He means, you're screwed," Maddock interrupted. "Ever heard the phrase *no honor among thieves?*"

"You shut your mouth!" Birdwatcher demanded.

Rossi turned to Birdwatcher. "I don't like the particular words he chose, but he's right, I'm afraid. Your services are no longer required."

Two of Virtuoso's men turned their weapons on Birdwatcher. The assassin grudgingly held his hands in the air. Two more men stepped forward and held their weapons on Maddock. A fifth man collected the fallen pistols.

"What the hell are you up to?" Birdwatcher growled. "We had an arrangement—a contract. What's this all about?"

"Let's just say we are terminating our contract with… extreme prejudice," Rossi said. "Get down on your knees and place your hands on top of your head. I'll deal with you in a bit."

Birdwatcher glared at Rossi but didn't move.

Rossi aimed his revolver at Birdwatcher's forehead. "You think I'm messin' around? I said, on your knees—now!"

He cocked his weapon.

Birdwatcher slowly dropped to his knees and laced his fingers together behind his head. "This is not over, Rossi. No one screws me over and gets away with it. I mean it!"

"Yeah, yeah, yeah," Rossi replied dismissively, feigning boredom. "I'm scared and all that. Whatever. Shut your yap."

He turned to Maddock. "You're the famous treasure hunter?"

"And you're Virtuoso."

"Just call me Anthony," he said, "or Mr. Rossi if you prefer. That whole nickname thing was fun at first but now...not so much." He looked Maddock up and down. "I've heard a lot about you—even saw your picture once but it was taken years ago, when you were a Navy SEAL. Frankly, I expected more of a buffed-up body-builder type," he continued. "You're smaller than I thought you'd be."

"The camera puts on ten pounds," he said.

"I'll cut to the chase. How would you...like to work for...me?" he said.

"Work for you?" Maddock replied. "Not interested."

Rossi held both hands apart, palms up, forming a look of faux shock on his face.

"Not interested?" Virtuoso repeated.

Maddock inclined his head toward Birdwatcher.

"Your retirement plan leaves something to be desired."

"He says he ain't interested," Rossi said. He looked at a couple of his men and smiled.

The men chuckled knowingly.

He turned back to Maddock and lowered the gun, slipping it into his coat pocket. "Well, I must tell you, that hurts my feelings."

"It's nothing personal," Maddock said. "Think of me like Superman, seeking truth, justice and the American way—that sort of thing."

"Oh, I get it—you're a *principled* man, right?"

Maddock shrugged. "Something like that."

"I did a little research on you," Virtuoso said. "I think you're a very smart man. You know what I do when I run into a very smart man?"

"I'm certain you're going to let me know," Maddock replied.

"I give them their options," Virtuoso continued. "Smart men do love their options. I have two options for you. Option number one: we kill you, your best friend and the woman. Then we bury the three of you in the woods and leave you for worm food."

Maddock said nothing—just stared at Rossi.

He looked at Maddock and grimaced. "Not a very attractive option, is it?"

"I'll go out on a limb here, but I'm thinking it won't be my first choice."

"Right. Now, in my humble opinion option two is the way to go," he continued. "You help me find the treasure, I'll give you ten percent of whatever is inside, and you three leave New York and go back to your lives a whole lot richer than when you started. Ten percent of several million dollars is a lot of money."

Maddock remained silent.

Rossi turned back to his men. "This guy is just like my wife. When I want her to shut up she runs her mouth like a motorboat. When I ask her for a decision, she can't make up her mind."

Rossi's men laughed, heartier than before.

After a few seconds Rossi held out his hands, palms up. He waved his arms up and down as if balancing a scale. "So what do you think—death? Or alive and rich?"

Maddock said nothing.

The smile disappeared from Rossi's face. He retrieved the gun from his pocket and aimed it at Maddock's forehead.

Maddock remained quiet.

"You think I'm joking?" Rossi asked, waggling the pistol in Maddock's face.

"What time is it?" Maddock asked.

"What? You got an appointment?"

Maddock didn't reply.

Rossi squinted and glared at Maddock as if trying to figure out a complex puzzle. Finally, he sighed and looked at his watch. "It's a few minutes after noon."

"Hmmm. In that case, I think I'm going take door number *three*."

"What are you, a wise guy?" he snarled. "There is no option three?"

"There's always an option three," Maddock said.

"Okay smart guy, tell me, what is option three?" Rossi asked.

"Guys!" Maddock screamed loudly. "If you're out there, now would be a really good time to make an appearance."

A voice boomed over an electronic megaphone.

"Anthony Rossi, this is the FBI! Lay down your weapons!"

EIGHTEEN

Rossi spun around and instantly began firing in the direction of the voice on the megaphone. His men followed suit, also firing blindly in the same general direction.

Maddock dove behind the nearest maple tree as unseen FBI agents began to return fire. He saw one of Rossi's men fall and a second one cry out in pain, dropping to his knees holding his shoulder.

Maddock heard repeated gunfire and the sounds of bullets whizzing by in all directions. At least two stray bullets pelted the tree Maddock had taken cover behind.

Birdwatcher used the distraction to flee. Maddock watched as the Frenchman scooped up his weapon from the ground and ran. He was unusually fast for a man his age and size and disappeared into the thick woods in a matter of seconds.

More gunfire rang out. When Rossi saw yet another one of his men take a bullet in the shoulder he threw his hands into the air. "Okay! Okay!" he screamed. "We're done. We give up."

The voice boomed out again over the microphone.

"All of you, drop your weapons, take three steps back and lay down on the ground face first and place your hands behind your heads."

Rossi nodded at his men and they ceased fire. They laid down their weapons and dropped to their knees before laying on the ground, as instructed. Rossi tossed his pistol aside as well but remained standing. Maddock emerged from behind the tree. Rossi glowered at him.

Men in camouflage fatigues and body armor

emerged from the surrounding trees to converge on Rossi and his men.

"I'm not getting on the ground. I got bad knees," Rossi said, "and I just had this suit cleaned."

One of the FBI strike team men moved in and put Rossi down with a hard shove.

Another man in a dark blue windbreaker made a beeline for Maddock. "I'm Special Agent Daniel Dawes."

"Birdwatcher took off in that direction," Maddock yelled, pointing east. "He's armed."

Dawes turned his eyes toward another of his agents, who in turn selected three of the men in combat gear and took off in the direction Maddock had pointed.

Dawes leaned down close to Rossi.

"Anthony Rossi, you are under arrest," he said.

"Really?" Rossi replied. "You're not here to give me a medal?"

"Save the comedy routine for your lawyer," the agent fired back. "He'll be looking for a laugh, since I know he won't find your situation to be very funny."

Rossi looked to Maddock. "How did you arrange this little party?"

"I knew the Frenchman was following us. I found out late that he knew where we'd be today. A friend of mine alerted the FBI this morning that Birdwatcher and your boys would be here today. I have a few connections. We asked them to converge on this place hard at noon on the dot." Maddock glanced over at Agent Dawes. "Good timing."

"We aim to please," Dawes replied.

"How did you know I'd be with them?"

"I didn't. I knew Birdwatcher would be here. I was sure you'd send your own men as back up. The fact that you're here in person is purely a bonus."

"How did they find us in the woods so easily?" Rossi asked.

Maddock pulled a cell phone from his pocket. "When Birdwatcher wasn't where I thought he'd be I made a call to the FBI and left the line open," he said. "GPS technology is pretty accurate."

"This ain't over Maddock," Rossi yelled.

"Get him out of here," Dawes barked.

NINETEEN

The next few hours went by in a blur. The FBI shut down the museum and cleared out all the visitors and employees. Ambulances and firetrucks swooped into the station. Michelle, Bones and Maddock were separated and questioned. The FBI confiscated Michelle's copy of *Mary Poppins* and placed it into evidence.

Maddock had been questioned for an hour and a half by the FBI and was left to sit and stew in the administrative office of the train station. A lower-level agent brought him a sandwich and a cup of coffee.

The agent, who introduced himself as Gil Sanchez, stood a couple inches shorter than Maddock. Clean shaven, with dark hair and brown eyes, he was solidly built. After he placed the food and drink on the desk, he sat on a chair, across from Maddock.

"I understand Tamara Broderick vouched for you," Sanchez said, his deep voice reverberating through the confined space.

"That's good to know." Tamara Broderick, known as "Tam" to those close to her, was formerly of the FBI, now a CIA agent running a team called the Myrmidons. She and Maddock had worked together many times in the past.

Sanchez scratched his chin. "She's got quite a reputation," the agent continued.

Maddock kept his silence. If the agent was fishing, he wouldn't catch anything in these waters.

"She's been connected with some unusual conspiracies, crazy rumors." Sanchez looked around to see if anyone was within earshot, cleared his throat. "You know, I've been thinking about becoming a treasure hunter like you," he said in a soft voice.

"Is that a fact?" Maddock responded.

"Yeah, what's it like?" he asked, leaning forward.

"Sometimes it's a blast. The chase, the moment of discovery. A lot of it's tedious. You have to enjoy the research. And when we're out on the water, working a grid, it's like finding a needle in a haystack. A lot of our work is done at sea."

Sanchez nodded. "I've lived at the beach. Done a lot of boating. Ever encounter any sharks?"

"Here and there. No great whites."

"What are those really dangerous jellyfish?"

"Box jellyfish. They're one of the top ten most dangerous creatures in the world. They're beautiful but in Australia, they call them sea wasps. They are responsible for more deaths than crocodiles, snakes and sharks combined."

"Holy crap!" Sanchez sat back, took a breath. "So, what advice would you give a beginning treasure hunter?"

"Don't be one." Seeing this was not the answer Sanchez was looking for, Maddock went on. "But if you're determined, you need as much capital as you can amass. Findings can be few and far between. Get a good crew around you, and learn as much as you can about the various aspects of archaeology. Being a history nerd helps, too."

"Thanks. Sorry if that seems a little unprofessional. I just haven't met a genuine treasure hunter before. One who's actually found things, I mean."

"It's not all it's cracked up to be. There's a lot of failure involved. And sometimes, you run into trouble."

Sanchez laughed. "I can see that. I've been in law enforcement all my life. Tactical team sniper, self-defense instructor. I can handle myself."

"Good to know." Maddock changed the subject. "If I've answered all your questions, when can I leave?"

"It shouldn't be too much longer." Sanchez reached into his pocket, took out a business card, and scribbled on the back. "That's my personal email address and cell. If you're ever in my neck of the woods again and need some help, I'll see what I can do." He turned and headed for the door. "There is one more agent who needs to speak with you."

The young man stood to leave.

Maddock ate his sandwich and drank his coffee, looking at the ancient, preserved office. On the bookcase, a row of binders caught his eye. There was a sign taped to the shelf above the binders. It was marked, "Acquisition Logs."

The binders were marked #1 through #9. Maddock pulled #2 at random. The last sheet was dated 3-11-1933. He replaced the paper, put the binder back in place, skipped over #3 and pulled #4.

Maddock began to leaf through it. It contained logs for 1935. The logs contained an inventory of the train equipment on display at the station along with the purchase and donation report.

As he leafed through the records a date caught his eye, September 19, 1935. It was a record of a purchase made of a decommissioned 1899 transfer caboose initiated by the owner—a man named Michael Banks. It was donated to the Phoenicia Train Station a month after it was purchased. Under purpose, the listing read, "additional office space." That was not a surprise to

Maddock. The station itself was small and he could see the benefit of using a stationary caboose as an extra administrative area. He also knew that many cabooses were used for offices in those days. On the right side of the page was a column used to notate a description of the caboose along with an identification number: Six-four-two.

A tall dark-skinned man with neatly cropped hair entered the room. He was trim but built solidly, wearing a dark suit and tie, giving him a distinct "Men in Black" look.

He wore a serious look on his face and pulled up a chair across the desk from Maddock. He flashed his credentials. "Thanks for waiting. Agent Dawes was nice enough to call me and let me know you were here. Sorry you had to be detained. I'm Agent Paul Travers. I'm with the Treasury Department. You are Dane Maddock?"

"Yes," Maddock said flatly.

Travers reached into his briefcase and pulled out the first edition of *Mary Poppins*.

"Tell me about this book, Mr. Maddock," Travers began.

"You're welcome," Maddock said.

"What?"

"I just wanted to say *you're welcome* for providing you information that led to the direct apprehension of Anthony Rossi. He's been on the FBI's Most Wanted list for what, three years now? I'm sure the Treasury Department had a vested interest in his capture, So, you're welcome for that."

Travers gave Maddock a dismissive chuckle. "At the moment, my interest is in this book."

"What is the nature of your interest?" Maddock

asked.

"At the time of his death, Dutch Shultz was wanted for bank robbery and tax evasion, among many other criminal acts. I am told this book might provide clues as to where his valuables may be stored. The Treasury Department would be highly interested in gaining restitution for some of the theft and financial fraud committed by Mr. Schultz."

"I see," Maddock replied. "Well, as you well know, there has never been a single shred of actual evidence that any treasure was actually hidden. Thousands—perhaps tens of thousands—of treasure hunters ranging from skilled professionals to rank amateurs, have tried their hand at finding it. No one of them has been successful."

Travers smiled for the first time. "Thank you for the history lesson. Mr. Maddock, but let's not play games. I've heard all about you. You wouldn't be here if there wasn't something to find. Your background is very colorful: lost cities; prehistoric artifacts; ancient shipwrecks filled with gold; unraveling conspiracies. It's all very Indiana Jones, isn't it? Your success rate is very high from what I understand."

"But not a hundred percent. Not every mystery can be solved. The dead ends just never make the headlines." Maddock paused a beat. "Did you read the notes in the margins by Dutch Schultz?"

Travers nodded. "I've spent the last hour reading them while Agent Sanchez was questioning you."

"And?"

"Did not understand one word," he admitted.

"There you have it," Maddock said.

"So, you've been here just over a week and you're

telling me ..."

"That coming to the Empire State Museum was a final straw, an act of desperation—a Hail Mary."

"And you haven't found the lost safe?"

"I have not."

"Mr. Maddock, do you know where the safe is?" Travers asked pointedly.

"I do not. Look, Agent Travers, *I called you guys.* Do you honestly think I would call you if I had anything to hide?"

"You might if you thought Rossi and Birdwatcher were going to kill you," Travers retorted. "When the FBI arrived, you were seconds away from death."

"Was I?" Maddock countered. "Rossi offered me a job. If I didn't know you guys were about to converge, I would have just bought some time by agreeing to work for him, and then improvised later."

"So, you weren't worried?" he asked.

"Worried is a relative term, isn't it?"

He held up the book and fanned the pages. "So all of this is ..."

"Who knows?" Maddock interrupted. "Check out the transcripts of Schultz's last words—they're public record. Almost none of it makes any sense. He wrote these notes the day of his death. He knew he didn't have long to live. He was under extreme duress. These notes were written to his mistress. It's possible some of them were written in code that only she and Dutch would understand."

"I'm not exactly following you," Travers said.

"It would be like someone saying, '*Meet me in the city mentioned in the song that was playing during our first kiss.*' If the song was '*Meet me in St. Louis,*' it would be impossible for anyone to know they were referring to the city of St. Louis other than the two people present at the time the song played."

"And it might even be St. Louis, Illinois." Travers let out a long sigh. "And you think these notes are that type of thing—things only Dutch and his mistress would have known?"

"I think it's possible," Maddock said.

"Mr. Maddock, are you playing me?" Travers asked.

"I'm just answering your questions, Agent Travers."

Travers held up the book again. "Because you know I could have you arrested."

"For what?" Maddock spouted. "Looking for Dutch's lost safe? I suppose you're then going to line up the tens of thousands of other hopefuls who have tried and failed and arrest them all?"

Travers paused and looked Maddock in the eyes. Finally, he let out a breath. "No," he said.

"So...are we done here?" Maddock asked.

Travers paused for a moment, then managed a small smile.

"We're done. You're free to go."

Maddock began to walk away.

"Oh, and Mr. Maddock?" Travers called out.

Maddock stopped.

"Thank you for the information leading to the arrest of Anthony Rossi."

"You're welcome. Did you catch the Birdwatcher?" Maddock asked.

"Nope, not yet, but it's a matter of time," Travers said. "Highway cameras spotted him getting into a Toyota Land Cruiser and heading north. We lost track of him, but we'll get him."

"I somehow doubt that," Maddock replied.

TWENTY

Maddock spent the next ten minutes summarizing his conversation with Agent Travers for Michelle and Bones.

"So, now you know what I know," he concluded.

"Look. The FBI—they're leaving," Bones said, peering out the window of the museum.

"Those bastards took my book," Michelle said, watching the procession of FBI vehicles roll away. "When did you even call them in?"

"When we first separated this morning," Maddock said. "I called Jimmy and told him Birdwatcher and Rossi's men would both be here and asked him to call the FBI and to have them to converge on the scene precisely at noon."

"Why noon?" Michelle asked.

"Calculated guess. I figured it would give us the time we needed to find the treasure if it were here."

"So much for that idea," Michelle said.

"How did you know Rossi would be here?" Bones asked.

"I didn't," Maddock admitted. "But, what I did know is that Rossi would not trust Birdwatcher to kill us and bring the treasure to him. Men like Birdwatcher and Rossi are cut from the same cloth—they trust no one. I knew Rossi would send his men for the money. I didn't count on him making a personal appearance, but it's all the better for the FBI. Us, too, really. I think they were so excited to nab Rossi, they've been less hard on us."

"This sucks," Bones said.

"What sucks, exactly?" Maddock asked.

"I mean, you know, all this that we've been through,

and now we'll leave empty-handed."

"Who said anything about leaving empty-handed?" Maddock asked.

"You just said yourself, Dutch's safe isn't here," Michelle said, confused.

"No, I said that's what I told the Men in Black," Maddock corrected.

"I'm not following you," Michelle said.

Bones smiled. "You found a clue, didn't you?"

"Yep. In the administrator's office."

A wide grin formed on Bones' face. "Tell us."

"Michelle, didn't you say you ran into an employee who'd been here for a long time?" Maddock asked.

"Yes, she said. "His name is Raymond. He's a sweet old bird, but he didn't know anything that could help us."

"Is he still here?" Maddock asked. "Can you find him?"

"When they swooped in, the FBI cleared the entire place out, employees and all," Bones said.

"The employees are trickling back in now," Michelle said. "I heard one of the agents talking to another. I guess they are going to let the museum reopen. I just saw Raymond walking by the window."

"Great," Maddock said. "Would you ask him if he'd mind joining us for a moment?"

Michelle walked to an open window and called for Raymond. Maddock watched as the elderly man approached.

"That was quite a bit of excitement we had here today, wasn't it?" he said to Michelle. "Everyone down here hit the ground when we heard gunshots."

"We're just glad no one got hurt," Michelle said.

"Did they get those boys who was doing the shootin'?" he asked.

"They did," Michelle said. "Raymond Wigg, I'd like you to meet my friend Dane Maddock."

Raymond extended his hand. "I'm pleased to meet you. I heard the FBI boys talking. You folks are looking for the lost treasure of Dutch Schultz?"

"We are," Maddock said, shaking the elderly man's hand. "Do you know anything about it?"

"Not firsthand, but I've heard stories. Always thought that treasure was up near Devil's Face someplace. I called Mr. Centerman. He's on the way."

"Who's Mr. Centerman?"

"Jeff Centerman. He's the Executive Director of the Catskill Center. He's also the Curator of this Museum."

"Dane has a question for you, Raymond," Michelle said.

"Okay, shoot."

"Mr. Wigg, I understand you've been around this place a very long time," Maddock asked.

"Yep, I have," he replied.

"There was an 1899 Ulster and Delaware transfer caboose donated here in 1935. The ID number is six-four-two. Is there any chance you know anything about it?"

The man nodded eagerly. "I sure do. Take a look out of the window. It's sitting outside, about a hundred feet from the station."

Bones looked through the window. "That one?" he said, pointing to the caboose.

"Yep," Raymond replied. "That's it. The way the story goes that car was bought and donated to the station for extra office space, but when it arrived it was locked up tight. The owner showed up a few days after it arrived and said he had changed his mind—he intended to move the car to Chicago, I believe."

"He was going to *move* the rail car?" Maddock asked.

"Yep, he wrote a letter to the station manager," Raymond said. "I've actually seen that note. I think it's in the office tucked in the binder marked 'Archived Transactions.' As far as I know, he never came back and efforts to find him failed."

"I'll go fetch the note," Michelle said, moving toward the office.

"It's the binder on the bottom shelf, toward the right," Raymond said.

"So, the owner never came back?" Bones asked.

"I don't think so," Raymond said. "What to do with that car has come up in many conversations off and on for years, even in the last ten years, but nothing has ever been decided. It's not bothering anything and it adds to the ambiance. It's been sitting there as decoration, collecting weeds ever since—untouched and unused."

"Unused? You're sure?" Maddock said.

"I've been looking at that number on the side of that caboose every day I've been here," Raymond said. "As far as I know that caboose has never been moved."

"Has anyone ever been inside of it?" Maddock asked.

"Oh sure," Raymond replied. "I've been in it once or twice myself. Nothing really to see in there. It's pretty well empty—maybe a couple of old chairs and desks."

"It's red," Bones noted, looking at the caboose through the window.

Michelle looked at Maddock. "*I love red*," she quoted from the book.

"What makes you believe the safe is in that particular

car?" Bones asked.

"In the log book, what first caught my eye was the day the caboose arrived at what was, at the time, the Phoenicia Train Station. It arrived on October 19, 1935. It was bought only a month earlier in Chicago and then transported here."

"October nineteen? That was four days prior to Dutch being killed," Bones said.

"Right," Maddock said. "And then I noticed the name of the donor—*Michael Banks.*"

"I found the book and the letter," Michelle said, returning. "It's hand-written. Here is the note to the Station Master, dated October 22, 1935. She read aloud, "*To whom it may concern, I am terribly sorry for the inconvenience, but I'm afraid I've made other plans for the transfer caboose. I will arrange for it to be retrieved and moved to Chicago by the end of the month. My apologies for the inconvenience. Respectfully, Michael Banks.*"

"He was going to move the caboose to Chicago," Maddock said.

Maddock took the note from Michelle and re-read it.

"But who is Michael Banks?" Bones asked, looking at Michelle. She flashed a knowing smile.

"You never actually read the book, *Mary Poppins*?" Maddock asked.

"Seriously, Maddock?" Bones asked. "Mary freaking Poppins?"

"Well, I read it when I was a kid…"

"Big surprise," Bones muttered.

"Anyway," Maddock went on, "one of the characters in the book, a child, is named Michael Banks. So, four days prior to Dutch Shultz's death, someone calling himself 'Michael Banks,' buys an old caboose, donates and delivers it to the Phoenicia Train Station. Three days later, Dutch passes through Phoenicia and the safe with his money disappears. It seems like more than just a coincidence."

"Michael Banks *was* Dutch Schultz," Bones said.

"I think so, yes."

"Remember one of the notes from the book said something to the effect of, *Have you ever been to Chicago? It's such a great town. I'd love to take you there one day.*"

"This letter to the Station Master is dated, October 22, 1935," Michelle said. "That's the day Dutch was said to have been in Phoenicia, one day before he was murdered."

"It makes sense," Bones agreed.

"Bear with me a second," Maddock said. "Here's what I think happened. Schultz feels the heat from the Mafia Commission and the FBI. He buys an old train caboose and has it shipped to the Phoenicia Train Station. He collects his money and valuables, drives to Phoenicia, puts them in the safe and hides it in the caboose, knowing full well he is going to have the rear car shipped to Chicago later. The money, of course, goes along for the ride."

"Wow," said Michelle. "That fits."

"He then locks the caboose up, writes the letter Michelle is now holding, and gives it to the Station Master," Maddock continues.

"He was planning to run away, wasn't he?" Michelle said. "He was going to take my great-grandmother with him."

"To Chicago, yes, I believe so. He loved her. He was

going to make an effort to disappear," Maddock agreed. "Maybe he was thinking he would tie up some details in Newark and head to Chicago, where this caboose...and the money, would be waiting."

"But he gets killed in Newark that night and never makes the final arrangements to move the caboose to Chicago," Bones said.

"And it's been here ever since," Maddock added.

"Wow!" Michelle said. "Well, what are we waiting for?"

"Michelle," Maddock began, "remember, this caboose has been out in the open in plain sight for over eighty years. If the safe ever was inside it, there's a strong possibility it was found and taken a long time ago."

"I don't believe it," she said. "No one had the information we have. Let's just go see."

Maddock looked at the caboose for the first time. It was faded red and ancient-looking. Except for the wheels and base, it was constructed of wood, now severely weathered and rotted. There was a wrought iron staircase leading to the door on the back end. The metal stairs had weeds and shrubbery growing through and all around it from years of neglect. There were three windows on the side; they were so covered in dirt and grime that nothing could be seen through them.

On top of the caboose was a loft with observation windows. Those were designed to be used so that an employee could observe load shifts as the train made turns around the bends.

"Mind if we have a look inside, Mr. Wigg?"

"I think it might be locked up. I don't believe I've even seen a key for it in ten years or more, but if you can get in...help yourself."

Maddock, Bones and Michelle approached the caboose and inspected the outside. The wood frame was severely dry rotted and bent. It looked as if it were ready to fall apart.

They climbed over the weeds to navigate the stairs. The door was locked and secured with a rusted padlock.

"Stand back," Maddock said stepping back himself. He braced himself against the back rail and gave to door a hard kick. The door held through his first two attempts and finally swung open on the third try.

A strong dank, musky smell rushed out of the caboose. The inside was dark and damp. Maddock saw a buildup of mold along the creases of the floor and ceiling. Beyond that ...

"It's empty," Bones said. "One chair, one desk."

Michelle opened the drawers of the desk. "Nothing. There's nothing in here."

"Now I know how Geraldo Rivera felt." Bones saw Michelle's puzzled frown. "You know, Al Capone's vault?" Bones turned his palms up in a plaintive gesture. "So...nothing?"

"Nothing that meets the eye...yet," Maddock admitted. "Then again, if it were in plain sight, someone along the way would probably have opened it just to see if there were any contents of historical interest. Maybe it's hidden."

Maddock systematically tested the floor and walls for some sort of false bottom or hollow space. He found nothing.

Bones went outside and inspected the perimeter of the caboose, testing it for hidden compartments, but soon came back in. He shook his head. He had found nothing.

"So, is that it?" Michelle asked. "You think someone else could have found it years ago?"

"That's always a possibility," Bones said.

"Let's check the loft," Maddock said.

An iron ladder attached to the wall led to the loft. Maddock climbed it. When he reached the observation deck, he groaned with disappointment. There was nothing there. He saw the severely stained windows and an empty desktop secured to the wall—that was it.

"What do you see?" Bones asked.

"Nothing," he replied. "Unless ..."

Maddock knocked on the wooden flat cover that served as the front facing of the desk. It was hollow.

"Unless what?" Michelle asked.

Maddock raised his right leg and kicked the front of the desk. The aged, dry wood crumbled easily and the desktop fell to the floor.

"What is it?" Michelle said as Maddock cleared the rotted wood away. He could hear her climbing the stairs.

Bones and Michelle made it to the loft as Maddock cleared the last of the rotted wood away.

And that's when he saw it.

A safe.

An ancient, rusty metal safe.

"Holy crap," Bones said, a broad smile splitting his face.

"Woo hoo!" screamed Michelle. She hugged Bones.

The safe was gun-metal gray in color, but time and oxidation had turned most of it reddish-brown. It was perhaps thirty inches tall and twenty-four inches deep. On the front was a gold leaf with *The Charpiot Safe Company, Denver Colo*, inscribed. Also, on the front was a combination wheel and a bronze handle.

"How do we open it?" Michelle asked.

"With the combination, of course," Maddock said.

"We don't have the combination," she said.

"We might, actually," Maddock replied. "I think Dutch created his own combination numbers and left it in the book."

"Dane, we don't have the book," she said. "The FBI does."

"That's okay," he said, pulling his cell phone from his pocket. "I took a picture of all the pages with notes, just in case. I think I have what we need."

He began thumbing through the photos on his cell. He held it up for Michelle to see. It was a picture of the inscription on the inside cover of the book. It read:

Happy Birthday

10-19-1910

I wish I could have kept you... safe.

The birthdate suddenly triggered in Michelle's mind.

"You think that my great-grandmother's birthday is the combination?" she asked.

"I do," Maddock said. "From the first moment I saw it, I thought it was odd that he would put your great-grandmother's birthdate in the inscription rather than the date he gave her the book, so I took a picture of it. Let's give it a whirl, shall we?"

Michelle and Bones both nodded.

Maddock stooped down and twisted the combination knob several times to the left. The knob was stiff and rusty but still moved.

"Left four times to ten, right three times to nineteen, left two times to nineteen, and right to ..."

Maddock heard a familiar click. He looked at Michelle. Her eyes were wide open; her mouth agape.

Maddock twisted the handle and heard the click of the bolt recession. He pushed the handle down and pulled.

With a loud squeak, the door came open.

Michelle gasped as Maddock opened the door to look inside.

TWENTY-ONE

Michelle drew in a sharp breath when her eyes fell on the burlap tobacco sacks. Bones patted her on the back gently. She seemed to recover quickly. Maddock opened one of the sacks. It was filled with twenty or more six-inch thick stacks of one-hundred-dollar bills, banded together. Another sack was filled with gold Liberty coins. There were six more burlap sacks and one eight by ten manila envelope.

Maddock retrieved the envelope and handed it to Michelle.

"You should do the honors but be careful. The paper is very old and fragile."

Michelle opened the envelope carefully. Inside was a tan stock certificate, now yellowed but in reasonable condition, issued by the Coca-Cola Company in 1933 for five shares of common stock.

Maddock took the certificate, examined the yellowed paper. Its cash value aside, he appreciated the historical aspect. He supposed he'd always be a history buff at heart.

"My God," Michelle said softly. "It's here; it's all here."

"And it's all the property of the United States Treasury Department," a deep voice called out.

Maddock turned to see the head of Agent Travers peeking into the loft from the top of the ladder.

"Back so soon?" Maddock said.

"I wasn't born yesterday," Travers fired back. "Come on down out of there, all three of you."

A group of armed agents stood outside the caboose.

All had serious expressions on their faces, save for Sanchez, who smiled and gave Maddock a single, knowing nod. Maddock winked.

A few minutes later Maddock, Bones and Michelle sat in front of Agent Travers in the same administrative office where he'd interviewed Maddock earlier.

"You lied to me, Mr. Maddock," Travers said. "You knew where the safe was all along."

"I didn't lie," Maddock argued. "While you all had me shut up inside this room, I found what turned out to be another clue. That clue didn't bear fruit until after you left. We had a chat with an employee, who helped us piece it all together."

"What made you come back?" Michelle asked.

"My intuition told me that Maddock was not done here," he said. "When we pulled away, I pulled off the side of the road and sat for a spell. When you didn't leave within the hour, I wondered what might be up, so I came back."

"And brought friends, I see," Maddock said.

Travers nodded. "I ran into Raymond Wigg—nice old fellow. He told me where you were."

"You know we already planned to turn the contents of the safe in," Michelle said. "This little demonstration of yours was not necessary."

"Yeah, this is not our first rodeo," Bones said. "We knew the Feds would have an interest in this safe's contents. You guys never miss a chance to take a nice big bite out of somebody's bank account. We would have called."

"Just out of the goodness of your heart, right?" Travers quirked an eyebrow.

"Common sense. We knew the Federal Government

would confiscate the cash and coins," Michelle said. "We expected that. But I'll point out to you that I'm a blood descendant of Dutch Schulz. In the book you took from us, you will see that Dutch willed everything he had to my great-grandmother. I am his rightful heir."

Travers stood. "That will be for the courts to decide."

"May I at least have my book back?" she asked.

"It's been booked into evidence," he said. "You'll get it back once this matter has been resolved."

"Why?" Bones protested. "We haven't committed any crime. The book is not evidence."

"Rossi was after the book. That makes the book evidence. A federal officer was wounded in that shootout today. Two of Rossi's men died. This is not a simple matter."

"That's a giant pile of crap," Michelle exclaimed.

"My advice to you is get a lawyer," Travers said. "A good one. You know the three of you are very lucky I don't arrest you and haul your asses off to jail, but I'm feeling mighty generous today. After all, you did something no one else in the world has been able to accomplish—you found the lost treasure of Dutch Shultz. And you helped us apprehend one of the top ten criminals in the U.S."

"Top five," Maddock corrected.

Travers smiled. "All of that carries weight. The Federal Government sends its regards. You all are free to go. We will undoubtedly see you in court."

Just as Travers stood a man appeared in the doorway. He was medium height and medium build, with glasses, short brown hair and full beard, just beginning to gray at the chin.

"Who are you?" Travers asked.

"My name is Jeff Centerman," he said. "I am the Executive Director of the Catskill Center and Curator of this museum. The safe in the caboose out front is on our property and is owned by the Catskill Center."

"That's ridiculous," Michelle said. "The caboose was owned by Dutch Shultz."

"Actually, the caboose, and its contents, were all owned by a donor named Michael Banks," Centerman countered. "There is no evidence that Michael Banks was an alias used by Dutch Schultz."

"Wrong again," Michelle huffed, holding up the letter. "This letter to the Station Master written in 1935 was written in Dutch Schultz's handwriting. It will prove not only that he was the rightful owner, but that he changed his mind and intended to move the caboose. That should be enough to prove this is not museum property."

"That *letter* is museum property," Centerman rejoined. "You must give it back. You had no warrant to search for it and no cause to take it. The same goes for the safe. It stays at the museum."

"Over my dead body," Michelle shouted.

Centerman turned to Travers. He looked at Michelle. "I'm afraid he's right about the letter, Miss. Give it back to him."

"Why? So, it will suddenly disappear?" she countered. "It's the only proof I have that ..."

"I'm sorry Miss, I must insist," Travers said. He turned back to Centerman. "As far as the safe goes, it is evidence of a crime committed here today. It goes with me...period."

"We will be prepared to fight for our rights," Centerman began.

"That's not my concern. Save it for the judge," Travers said. He turned to Maddock, Bones and Michelle.

"As you can see, this is probably going to get complicated. I wouldn't doubt that other interested parties pop up as well, perhaps the other descendants of Mr. Schultz. I'm sorry."

Maddock took the letter from Michelle.

"If that letter somehow gets destroyed ..."

"I have seen the letter," Travers said. "I can speak to its contents in a court of law."

"But the handwriting analysis would prove that Michael Banks was also Dutch Schultz," she said. "I need the actual letter for the handwriting analyst."

"Sorry, ma'am," Travers said.

"Expect a subpoena for that," Maddock said as Centerman took the document.

Centerman's brow furrowed but he kept his silence.

"You'll be hearing from us," Maddock said in a calm voice. Already his mental Rolodex was spinning, trying to think of people who could step in and provide assistance.

Travers fixed Maddock with a long, level gaze. "Go back to hunting for Bigfoot. You're out of your depth here."

Maddock bared his teeth in a wolfish grin. "We'll see."

TWENTY-TWO

Michelle had downed two glasses of Jack Daniels and vanilla Coke, and her eyes were looking a little unfocused. Bones had matched her gulp for gulp, while Maddock nursed a single beer.

"That could not have gone worse," Michelle said. "How about another round?" She waved her empty shot glass at Bones. "Uno mas tequila, por favor?"

"Maybe you should slow down," Bones said.

"Who are you, my mother? Just piss off." Michelle's chin fell to her chest and her eyelids drooped. Bones touched her shoulder in a consoling manner, but she brushed his hand away. "What am I going to do now? Go back to making chain mail armor for my dog to wear to renaissance festivals?"

"That actually sounds pretty cool," Bones said. "The armor, not the renaissance faire."

Michelle rolled her eyes.

"Hey, don't give up," Maddock said. "We knew all along the government was going to stick its nose in."

"I know," she said, "but my attorney and I had a plan. He said having the document in my possession would allow me to deal from a position of strength. We were going to turn over the cash and coins but keep the stock certificate. We would then let the feds know the certificate existed, and send a photocopy to them, but also, would notify them that I was laying rightful claim to it. That would put them in the position of trying to obtain it legally rather than the other way around." She paused, rubbed her eyes before continuing.

"If the government resisted, my lawyer was prepared

to take action—restraining orders; cease and desist; that kind of thing. He believed the government would look at the facts, decide it was an uphill battle, and let it go. The way it sets now, they have it and they will fight to keep it, and as we all know the federal government doesn't always play fair. And now I have the Empire State Museum to fight as well. I'm screwed."

Bones shrugged. "So sue."

"I don't have the money for a protracted legal battle," she said, head still hanging. I have to sue the government but first I'll have to get that letter from the Museum. That will be a legal tango that will last for months."

"This may help," Maddock said, showing Michelle a photo from his phone.

"What is that?" she asked.

"During all the hubbub, I snapped a photo of the letter that Dutch wrote to the Station Master," Maddock said, "just in case the original was ever...misplaced. The writing is crystal clear. You should be able to get a handwriting analyst to confirm the writing came from Schultz."

"Good thinking," Michelle said.

"I also have pictures of every page of the book containing a note from Dutch Schultz," Maddock said, "including the one where he says he wants your great-grandmother to have all he owns."

"That's huge," Michelle admitted. "Thank you, but it still doesn't change the fact I have no money to fight this with."

Maddock glanced at Bones. The twinkle in his friend's eye told him the suspicion he'd been harboring was correct. "I think you might be wrong about that."

"What do you mean?" she asked, raising red, watery eyes.

"Show her, Bones," Maddock said.

Bones reached into his pocket, withdrew two gold coins, and laid them on the table in front of her.

Confusion turned to glee as she gazed at the coins.

"Are those what I think they are?"

"Well, if you *think* they are two 1930-S twenty-dollar Regular Strike Gold Liberty Coins," Bones said, "then yes, they are what you think they are, and they're in perfect condition."

"You stole them from the safe?" she blurted.

Bones looked around the bar. Michelle's outburst had drawn the notice of a pair of men at a nearby table.

"You remember when you had your first beer, don't you?" he said to the men.

The pair smiled and returned to their conversation.

Michelle glowered at Bones.

"You...stole...the...coins," she repeated.

"Why don't you freaking Snapchat it?" Bones whispered back in an irritated tone. "Facebook and Twitter might want to hear about it, too. Yeah, I stole them for you. And there's a couple more in my pocket. It's an old habit I haven't managed to shake, not that I tried very hard."

"You took them for me?" she echoed.

"You'll need the money for your legal fight," Maddock said. "At auction, these coins, in mint condition have sold from anywhere between a hundred and a hundred-fifty grand. We won't be able to get quite that much for them, but Bones has connections that will pay you well for them and keep quiet about it."

"I don't know what to say." Tears welled again in her

eyes, but this time they were accompanied by the ghost of a smile. "Even after you take your share, that should be enough for the legal wranglings."

"We want you to have all the money," Bones said. "I'd just blow it in Atlantic City, anyway. Knowing my luck that little old Asian lady would still be there waiting for me."

"What about you?" she asked Maddock. "Are you sure you're okay with this?"

"Sure. It would just put me in a higher tax bracket if I kept it."

"Take it," Bones said. "Go sue the Feds."

"I can't believe this," she said.

Michelle was rendered mute by shock and gratitude. She hugged each of them tightly in turn. When she could finally speak, she insisted that Maddock and Bones keep one of the gold coins.

"What's next for the two of you now that this mystery has been solved?" she asked.

"Not sure," Maddock said, "but trouble always manages to find us."

"I won't forget this," she whispered.

"We'll be in touch once we've sold the coins," Maddock said.

Michelle gave Maddock another hug and gave Bones a kiss that wasn't quite chaste.

They watched as she walked out the door.

Bones was silent for a moment, then said, "You think Birdwatcher is still on our trail?"

"When I got to my room last night, I found this lying in the middle of my bed," Maddock replied. He slid a Payday candy bar wrapper across the table.

Bones let out a long, slow breath. "You never saw

him, though?"

"Nope," Maddock said. "He was delivering a message."

"And the message was?"

"A warning," he said. "A mind game. He wants me to believe he can find me at any time. Who knows? Maybe he can."

"You gonna call the FBI?" Bones asked.

Maddock shook his head. "What good would it do?"

"Well, if you should decide to take the fight to that asshat, you know I'm in."

"I'm counting on it."

Bones raised his glass. Maddock picked his up and clinked it.

"Cheers."

Bones smiled. "Another adventure. Another treasure we didn't get to keep. Another chick walking out of our lives."

Maddock nodded. "It's what we do."

The End

ABOUT THE AUTHORS

David Wood is the USA Today bestselling author of the action-adventure series, The Dane Maddock Adventures, and many other works. He also writes fantasy under his David Debord pen name. When not writing, he hosts the Wood on Words podcast. David and his family live in Santa Fe, New Mexico. Visit him online at davidwoodweb.com.

Stephen John has been writing professionally since 1993. He is the author of five novels which reached number one in Amazon KindleWorld's bestseller list for *Action and Adventure* or *Mystery and Thriller*: *Out With a Bang*, *Fortune and Fame*, *Fortune and Glory*, *Fortune and Pride*, and *Devil's Face*. He has also written *The Journey of Peter McCall*, a prequel to the Wayward Pines trilogy, and "The Muse of Malumere," a science fiction short story. Stephen lives in Seattle, Washington. When he's not writing, he spends his spare time with his family, plays classic rock on his acoustic guitar and enjoys his role as a parent and grandfather..